AFTERMATH

A tale of a family's survival

T.A. Walters

Aftermath Book 1 Copyright © 2019 by T.A. Walters.
All rights reserved. No part of this book may be reproduced in any form or by any electronic or mechanical means including information storage and retrieval systems, without permission in writing from the author. The only exception is by a reviewer, who may quote short excerpts in a review.

Cover designed by Bin de Vinner XII, PhD, Esq.

This book is a work of fiction. Names, characters, places, and incidents either are products of the author's imagination or are used fictitiously. Any resemblance to actual persons, living or dead, events, or locales is entirely coincidental.
T.A. Walters. Visit my website at
https://www.TA-Walters. com
Printed in the shade of the United States of America
First Printing: January 2019
ISBN: 9781793006073

AFTERMATH

CHAPTER 2

~forgotten~

There was no Chapter 1.

America came to a stop the instant Winston and his wife, and two kids stepped through the doors of a store wheeling a shopping cart loaded with the week's groceries. Unaware of an ECM's (Electrical Counter Measure) a counter-strike missile's failure to bring down an Inter-Continental Ballistic Missile aimed as a first strike attack from somewhere off in the third world, misfired and exploded over the eastern half of America. The ICBM, left unchallenged unleashed a high altitude wide-range nuclear explosion, triggering a massive EMP force that reaped destruction on all electrical devices. Unbeknownst to Winston and his family, missile Defense Networks scrambled to rediscover one another as did many military satellites which inadvertently lost track of Earth.

Less than eight minutes later, explosions rocked the skies overhead. Both ICBMs with wide range nuclear warheads and equipped with altitude limiters deployed their payloads in a precise measure, knocking out electrically sensitive equipment. Larger and more massive was the damage to the nation's three main power grids. Giant electrical generators screeched to a stop as the internal winding fried. The windings fraying out and jamming the generators under such extreme force they literally exploded under the relentless forces which drove them.

* * *

Everyone remembers where they were and what they were doing when the power went out for a day or two. Such was not the case when the days dragged on for months and now, over a year. Not unlike everyone else Winston had formerly held down a job to support his family and their way of life. Now it seemed that old way of life was just a game parlayed by the distortion of some wild fantasy. Nowadays, nothing comes that easy.

Supporting his family now was a full-time job in ways that remained with him from sunup to sundown. Foraging for food took most of his thoughts, and there were days when clean rainwater went short, wild game congregated to parts unknown. In short, despite Winston's best efforts, hunger ran hard in the small town near Alligator Alley Florida. The entire population of Hartley was nearly two thousand people, but as Winston would suggest if asked; the community of Hartley was now fewer than half.

For every man and, in every woman's life, there is a turning point. Most are driven by a need to adapt, or subject from a dramatic event in one's life. Winston was inspired by both. He could no longer bear to watch his wife and two young children wither away from starvation.

Years before, Winston relished the idea that someday he too could move up in life through hard work. He watched as others drove new cars and lived in houses that didn't leak rain. Perhaps it was a Godsend that he was poor. If it weren't for the consolation that no one robs poor people, he wouldn't now be considered wealthy. He had a truck and a car that actually ran when none of the newer vehicles would. He had all the gasoline he could gather from dead vehicles along the highway. In his old truck, Winston carried several 5-gallon gas cans, and with his hose and punch bit, he'd tap the gas tanks of all the abandoned vehicles from several miles in either direction from his family's home. The addition of a shut-off valve inline of his hose and punch bit made transferring gas easy. Except for the one day while under a car an alligator decided to join him and reveal to him a secret.

Being of Indian descent didn't mean Winston was superstitious and animal spirits could communicate wise exposés of knowledge, no. Through eye to eye contact, the big reptile told him, to survive he had to revert to the ways of his ancestors. Winston had to move in the tradition of the Seminole Indian. The dependency of he and his family relied on more than just what was stored in canning jars and fish that he would bring home. There were many resources left untapped and in his shed were stored away some of the finest camping gear many could only hope for. Those days of gathering fish and squirrel and expecting the government would return were over. There were no sheriff's departments, no ambulances, fire departments – nothing. All the people who ran them are home foraging a life for their own families and loved ones. The system of monetary compensation as was the entire economy had collapsed. There were no dollars. No paychecks. No incentives to go on being a policeman, a firefighter or even a mechanic like him and the others he had worked with at the auto dealership in Miami. Someday, he thought, he would venture into town and see if his chest of tools were still there and if so, he would collect them and bring them back home to his shed where they belong.

For now, Winston knew he would have to focus on the skills his grandfather taught him as a kid growing up. Winston grew up to love camping and had accumulated much in the way of camping equipment. Borrowing from the 'old ways' to the new, his grandfather showed him how to build above ground campsites

AFTERMATH

complete with sleeping platforms called a 'Chickee,' and natural remedies for illness and injury including mosquito repellents. It was amazing all the things he had collected on the way to where he was now, a full grown man with a family. When Winston showed an interest in archery, his grandfather was there to cheer him along. He told him it was a skill he would never forget, like riding a bicycle or walking on stilts. Once learned it was yours to keep, his grandfather would tell him.

And learn he did. Winston even learned how to make his own arrows and maintain all the things that were important to him in survival. He learned how to set traps for wild game and how to hunt and bring down even the largest of wild hog. All this and more were the ways life as it were in the beginning. Winston realized that it had been a year now and things were going to get worse when it came to survival. He knew it was time to say goodbye to the diminishing light of modern ways.

For the next few days, Winston focused his mind on the words and ways of his grandfather. Perhaps it was the spirit that came to visit him that day in the form of an alligator. With each day that passed, Winston became closer to his Indian heritage. He felt he'd become balanced in a feeling hard to describe. It was not that he thought indifferent to change, he was proud of what he'd become. He was a man of modern skills as equal in the nature of the ancient ways of his heritage taught to him by his father and grandfather. Such was the contemporary side of him that told him the gasoline he had been gathering lately was quickly becoming stale. His pickup truck was becoming intolerant to the old petrol he collected and would often spit and sputter when the engine was started and cold. The time had come to visit his former workplace at the dealership and fetch his tools and a few bottles of fuel extender he kept in the drawer beneath his workbench. The trip into Miami was one that Winston dreaded the most these days. He knew the people there were desperate for food and probably dangerous. He feared there would be the chance he would not return home, and so, he spent the next few days trapping game and fishing so that his family would have food while he was away.

CHAPTER 3

Winston was busy clearing out items in his shed that he felt he didn't need. Those items were loaded into his pickup truck. To make room, he removed all but one gas can from his truck, the others he stored in his shed. Duplicates of things like saws, hammers, and shovels were carefully stacked in his truck with the idea that he had to leave room for his tools when he got to the dealership in Miami.

Winston's wife Mary ran up to the shed from the house with a basket of canned fruit, salted jerked pork and a large sack of sugar and rock candy – all homemade from the sugar cane that grew nearby. Joseph and Darby stood close to either side of their mother. Darby was only 5 years old, and she was as beautiful as her mother in a lot of ways – smart too. Joseph was the eldest of the two children at the age of 10 and often stuck close to his father, but not today. Winston feared it was too dangerous to take him along with him to Miami, so Winston did the best he could to persuade Joseph he needed to stay home and watch over things until he returned.

Winston reached through the door of his pickup truck and pulled down the Marlin lever action 30/30 from the gun rack at the rear window. Joseph was a big boy for his age and didn't flinch a muscle when he grabbed the 7-pound rifle from his father's hand. "It's up to you to protect the household," Winston told Joseph.

"Yessir," Joseph responded quickly.

Winston stared at his son. How quickly Joseph had grown, he thought, drawing a deep breath, while at the same time being confident everything would turn out okay. "Just a little reminder son," he said smiling. "Bullets are scarce these days, no shooting unless it's absolutely necessary."

Joseph nodded. He already knew that from the days his father took him out practice shooting. The 30/30 had a bit of a kick to it, and the crack of the bullet was a sound that made his ears buzz for what seemed like an hour, but he loved shooting a gun nonetheless. Joseph loved shooting his dad's Model 500 Mossberg Shotgun. They had plenty of shells of all kinds in the house. The birdshot was easy for him to shoot, but the cartridges loaded with buckshot would nearly make him take a seat on the ground!

Joseph's eyebrows rose as he glanced up at his dad, "Shouldn't you be taking the shotgun?"

AFTERMATH

Winston smiled back at Joseph, "It's behind the seat, but keep in mind son; this will be no more different than those days I went off to work and returned the same day. So I expect to see your mother and Darby in a couple of hours. Okay?"

Joseph nodded. His father was right.

* * *

As Winston drove away, seeing his family and home framed in his rear-view mirror slowly disappear, he couldn't help the feeling that he may not return. Over and over in his mind, he wrestled with a conscience that questioned his motives. *Was this trip to Miami really necessary? Was what he hoped to gain from his trip worth the risks?* After all, what Winston hoped to do was merely regain what belonged to him and nothing else. That is if his personal belongings were still at the dealership. Should they still be there he would gladly use the items he loaded in his truck to barter with on the advent someone challenged his resolve for reclaiming his tools and bottles of fuel extender.

He checked his trouser pocket for the ring that had the dealership machine shop key on it. Inside the machine shop were a brake turning lathe and a floor press for such things as removing and reinstalling rear axle bearings and other things. However, most importantly was his second chest of tools. Winston was comforted by the idea that if his workbench tool chest in his lift bay area were stolen, at least the one locked inside the machine shop would still be there.

After nearly two hours of driving, Winston looked at familiar places he remembered over a year ago. Having passed Miami's International Airport, he recalled how it only took an hour to get to work. Taking double that time because of road obstruction mostly from dead vehicles added that extra time that he would have otherwise driven at high speed. Although there were familiar places, they were not the same. Most all were vacant, and some business's looked like bombed-out buildings straight out of a war movie. Most windows looked smashed, and many homes and businesses had chicken wire, barbed wire or even chain link fencing that looked as if hastily installed around a few houses and shops. It was an eerie sight to see. Winston had never seen this place along Brown Dairy Road to look so desolate before. Everything was overgrown with tall dead grass. He was used to seeing cracks in the highways teeming with weeds and grass, but such sights as vines and kudzu taking over some businesses in a way that looked as if the jungle was slowly encroaching upon the City of Miami.

Winston slowed down and looked around for anyone moving about the avenues and byways, alleyways – anywhere. All he saw were matted clothing on the streets and sidewalks here and there. The population in this area seemed limited to a few dog packs he'd seen. One such dog, mangy and painfully thin, wrestled a bone that lay hidden in a matted pile of clothing. Winston swallowed hard in the realization that the piles of clothing were what remained of the people who stayed behind. Perhaps the balance of people left for the city. This, being the 'outskirts' of the city and the area where the car dealership was, put Winston's mind at ease knowing that human contact would undoubtedly be limited if at all.

Turning off Brown Dairy road on to Bessard Avenue North, Winston drove up to the dealership service entrance. Instead of driving up to his service lift bay, he pulled the truck off the side of Bessard Avenue and got out to check on the fence gate lock. He wrestled with the work keys on his keyring. He had been issued several keys from the dealership, many of which, he never used. The gate padlock was one of them. It was a large chrome padlock, heavy and made by American Lock Co ™. With all the keys he had, one stood out from all the rest; a key engraved with the logo: American Lock ™. Winston breathed a sigh of relief seeing the key slip into place. It was as if the padlock had been opened recently or at least lubricated not long ago. The tumbler lock assembly turned smoothly, and the hasp jumped up with a metallic click. A ½ inch chain of a length of about 4 feet secured the gate to the padlock. Once removed, Winston carefully reattached the padlock into one link of the chain and allowed it to dangle on the gate post. The gate itself hinged on one side while the other side rolled along the ground on a hard rubber tire, so as Winston swung the gate open he noticed contrary to the condition of the lock, this gate had not been swung open in ages. He studied the tire tread on the dirt covering the once clean concrete driveway. His opening of this gate was the first time in perhaps months, maybe even a year.

Winston climbed back into his truck, grabbed a large chunk of jerky and a string of rock candy and stuffed it in his right hip pocket for later. Once past the gate, he turned to stop by the door of the machine shop, noticing as he did, the door closed and locked. He shut off his truck and decided to check inside the machine shop for his tool chest. The only other sound that broke the silence now was the familiar sound of the slide action on a pump style shotgun at the back of his head.

AFTERMATH

CHAPTER 4

It had been three days since his father left for Miami and now Joseph lies shivering in a ditch across the road from his house. Occasionally Joseph leaned up to get a glimpse of his home where no activity could be seen. He believed the two strangers were still inside along with his Marlin 30/30 rifle. He hoped by now they hadn't found the rifle he kept under his bed.

It had been several hours now, and no sound from within the house. Earlier there had been screaming, yelling and the agonizing wailing of his mother and sister. They had come without warning from somewhere, perhaps on foot. Joseph had gotten a good look at them, and there were two of them. Both of them were about the same size, though one was fatter than the other and had lots of tattoos on one of his arms. The other man had black teeth and a crazy look in his eyes. Joseph assumed they had pistols but wasn't entirely sure of that. There had been no gunshots, and before things got quiet, there were lots of yelling and screaming.

Joseph once again cried. This was his entirely *his* fault. He shouldn't have left the house to rummage for radishes in the garden without taking his rifle with him. With that thought, triggered a flurry of ideas in Joseph's head. Many times in the past his father would tell him to 'think before you leap,' and never embark on an idea without coming up with a plan first. Father would always say, "Plan your work and work your plan." Sniffing back the tears, Joseph thought over a plan. Again, he didn't know whether the strangers were armed or not but judging by the sound of his mother and Darby's screams, it was a sure bet that they were. Whatever business they had here was unknown to Joseph, but he felt they had overstayed their visit, so sneaking through the back window of his bedroom to gain access to his rifle was the dominant plan that Joseph entertained. Of course, that would have to wait until nightfall.

Joseph tried to brush away the idea that a failed rescue attempt could mean the death of his mother and sister and in the end him as well. Nonetheless, it would have been precisely the plan his father would follow. Convinced the plan he devised had little chance of failing, Joseph never recalled how quickly the remaining daylight hours could slip away so fast.

* * *

In the balmy evening air, crickets chirped along with a chorus of croaking frogs. Joseph crept through the tall grass for the house occasionally stopping when the night singers detected his presence. It was important that the crickets and frogs continued their night time singing less giving away his position if they suddenly stopped.

His advance around to the back of the house took nearly an hour; however, when he got there, he saw the back door standing wide open. He slowly rose to his feet. The back door led into the kitchen and living room. His bedroom window was on the far end of the house opposite the kitchen door. Joseph usually kept his window open all day and night this time of the year when the summer heat was about. Darby's room had no windows and was partitioned off in the pantry to make her a place to sleep. Mother and father had a bedroom on the opposite side of the kitchen wall, leaving a modest living room space out front. The front door of the living room led out to a large porch outside.

Climbing through his bedroom window as quietly as possible, Joseph paused by the window looking down at the floor. He knew things about this house most take for granted, such as where the squeaky floorboards were, and where they weren't. So stepping across the floor to his bed where the rifle was hidden underneath, there were two distinct areas where the floor would creak and moan. The only way to get close to his bed was to follow along with the wall, which also meant going from one wall to the other adjoining wall and then two steps forward to the side of his bed nearest the headboard. Without further thought, Joseph found himself silently counting out the footsteps until finally he slowly knelt at the headboard and ducked his head down to peer underneath his bed. Handicapped by the darkness, he could only slowly wave his arm under the bed. Hoping to get a feel of his rifle, his hand swept a toy truck out from underneath the bed making a scraping noise as it landed on its side skidding across the floor. His heart nearly leaped from his chest as he quickly stretched his body flat and face down to the floor scuttling in beneath the bed as quickly as he could. Joseph's left arm hit something hard, and as he ran his hand down the length of it, he discovered the feel of his rifle. With the thought of having his rifle, he felt as if he'd grown ten feet tall. However, Joseph had the patience to lie still and wait; silently listening to any sounds that may result from his toy truck scraping across the floor earlier. He waited for any sound; floor creaks, the rustle of clothing, breathing – anything.

Joseph was alerted by the soft hymn of a mosquito around his ear. Soon, the hymns of a dozen or more mosquitoes joined in, and it became apparent that the house had not been fogged for the evening. In fact, it seemed as if it took several minutes for the mosquitoes to find him, lending him to believe that he was alone in the house. There was not the lingering smell of palmetto and camphor smoke left

AFTERMATH

behind from fogging the house. Joseph knew folks in the area always knew to fog before nightfall, or the mosquitoes would become unbearable as they have now. He began to doubt anyone was here in the house to attract mosquitoes until he came in.

Another plan.

Joseph needed another plan to determine his next move. He needed a way to determine if the bad men were still in the house and that meant whether or not his sister and mother were in the house as well. Trying to figure out their motives for invading and attacking his family, Joseph only knew times were hard that they were out foraging for food, and what better place to come here where the picking is easy. He could not recall hearing shots fired – but the screaming still echoed in his head.

Did they beat up his mother and sister? Were they here lying unconscious in the living room?

The more Joseph thought about these things, the more he persuaded himself to slowly move to the living room.

Scooting out from under the bed, he slowly crept to his bedroom door and stood there in the dark, his Marlin 30/30 in his hands almost ready for action. *Almost ready,* was the term his father taught him; a fishing pole was almost ready when it was loaded with bait, but not until it is cast out on the water is it fishing. An arrow nocked on the bowstring is almost ready, but not until the bowstring is pulled back is it ready, and so it is for a rifle when it is almost ready but really *not prepared* to fire until it has chambered a live round and it is cocked.

Much more than cocking the lever action on his rifle and chambering a 30 caliber round was the steely shuffle that broke the silence, echoing out into the living room was the fact he was there. Worse was the thought that he would be seen first, and taken down the moment he appeared in the living room. Maybe even shot.

Somewhere off, he heard a noise that sounded as if it came directly ahead of him. His finger tightened against the trigger waiting for the sound or the sight to become familiar to him as being his mother or sister.

The hairs of the back of his neck all the way down to his arms stood electrified in fear of what was about to come his way.

"Who's there?" asked Joseph.

There was no reply, just a sound that increased in volume.

CHAPTER 5

It, being a shotgun held against the back of his head bereft Winston with any thought except one. *Do exactly what this person wants.*

"Put your hands where I can see 'em," snarled the gunman.

Winston slipped the keys in his trouser pocket and then slowly raised his hands. "I used to work here."

"I bet you did," replied the gunman sarcastically.

"I'm Winston Sawyer, and I was a mechanic here before the economy collapsed."

"Turn around ... slowly."

When the man's face came in to view, Winston tried to recall whether he had seen this gentleman before. "Do I know you?"

"Shut up. I'll be the one asking questions." The gunman turned a glance toward the fence and waved his shotgun in that direction. "Walk over there slowly and lock that gate back the way you found it."

Winston did precisely what he was told, and while doing so, he asked, "Are you the security guard here?"

He heard the man bellow forth a laugh that echoed through the partially open space of the service bay area, "Security? Why the hell no. I took over this place shortly after the crash. I scaled that fence, taking my puppy with me and this here shotgun."

Finishing with securing the gate, Winston turned to face the gunman. The man's dog was obediently sitting at the feet of the gunman and staring at Winston. "That's a big dog you got there."

"Yep, takes big bites too."

"I've got to admit, I didn't even hear him come up here."

"He's a Rottweiler. Name's Rustler. He doesn't bark. He's just interested in people is all."

"Interested in people?"

"Yep, he eats them."

"Really, you're serious?"

"Yep. Rustler's favorite bone is inside your leg."

AFTERMATH

Winston was too afraid to consider the obvious. Having a dog nearly the size of a Shetland pony meant having to feed him large amounts of food. Times being what they were, Winston wondered where this old gunman got the food to feed Rustler.

Winston bit his lip. "So do you let Rustler outside this place to hunt his own food ... or what?"

"I don't like where you're going with these questions," he told Winston. "How about you start walking to that door across the way."

Before the gunman could react, Winston tugged free his pork jerky slab and held it out to Rustler. Rustler seemed reluctant, but took the jerky and gobbled it down in three bites. "He likes rock candy too!"

"Back away!" the gunman warned waving his shotgun in Winston's face. Winston grimaced when he saw the gunman kicking Rustler in the chops. He continued to kick Rustler in the ribs over and over while the dog yelped with each kick. Winston struggled to find a way to divert the gunman's attention away from brutalizing poor Rustler.

"I notice you have a police badge pinned to your ball cap. Were you a cop?"

They walked along slowly as the gunman explained, "If you must know, and I don't see no harm in it, no I ain't no cop and never was."

"Well if you got the badge and the riot shotgun, where's the cop that it belonged to go?"

He huffed and then replied, "Ask Rustler. A cop came in one night looking around I suppose. Found this stuff the next morning out in the driveway along with the bones Rustler was teething on when I found him."

Winston's eyes widened, "You're shitting me right?"

"Rustler might be shitting you tomorrow, but I never would."

It was hard to tell if this man was on the level, but deserving a nervous laugh, Winston remarked, "So what do you eat?"

"Leftovers."

Winston swung open the door to the customer's lounge and entered holding the door for the gunman who gave Rustler a swift kick in the ribs. Rustler yelped out in pain and then turned a whine into a growl as his furry brow flattened along the ridge of his eyes while snarling with bared teeth.

The gunman then turned to Rustler, "I done told you a million times you ain't allowed in here until I open the door for you, now git before I hang you on a hook!"

The gunman turned to Winston and yelled at him to sit in a chair next to a vending machine that had long been smashed and looted. Seconds later the gunman slapped a pair of police handcuffs on Winston's left wrist and cuffed him to the chair he was sitting in. All around him were the disgusting remnants of dried blood and fragments of flesh. *No wonder he didn't want Rustler to come in here.*

T.A. Walters

Sitting across from a window that Winston remembered as the customer side of the automobile parts counter, he watched as the gunman hopped up onto the counter and slide down on the other side. He remembered years before, the attic storage space above the parts room and the shallow stairway leading up to it. Somewhere in that darkened storage space was where the gunman called home. Winston recalled the handcuff key stuck to the handcuff as if it were magnetized. Keeping his eye on the gunman the whole time suggested to him that the key never went into his pocket. Not even when he hopped over the parts counter with it still in his hand. Between that time and the time he reached the attic stairway, the key appeared missing from his hand. Or it was placed somewhere behind the counter. *Could the key have been placed on a magnet?*

* * *

Winston awoke several times throughout the night. Left handcuffed to the chair nearest the vending machine, he knew there was no place to go. The seat he was sitting in was mounted on an extended framework of metal tubing with several other seats bolted to it. Attempting to escape was impossible as well as moving around the lounge without trying to drag with him a few hundred pounds of metalwork with him. The idea of moving across the room to the parts counter might be doable except for the racket it would make as he bumped and scraped along the floor and over a large coffee table situated in the middle of the room. If he could get to the parts counter, he was confident the handcuff key was within reach somewhere along the inside edge of the counter itself.

A row of seats made up his bed, and getting comfortable was impossible as the edge of each seat dug into him. At times he woke up hearing strange noises coming from the upstairs attic. It sounded like the muffled sound of voices. At one point in the night, Winston caught a glimpse of the gunman leaving the lounge, shotgun in hand, only sometime later returning to his attic hideout.

When the sun rose and the customer lounge filled with sunlight, Winston was released from his chair and allowed to use the bathroom. The washroom facility was filthy and dank and had no windows. Also, the toilet was full and because it was nearly overflowing Winston choked up what little remnants his stomach held.

Head foggy and his throat parched, Winston quickly discovered there was no water to wash with or drink. He soon realized the madman that held him the prisoner had the intentions of killing him. It was coming down to a decision of life or death consequences, and Winston had never killed anyone before; however, he feared that he would have to consider killing this madman if he were to come through this alive. He also knew the minute he left the bathroom he might be killed,

AFTERMATH

or possibly later at some point. The element of surprise could be in his favor if it weren't that the gunman always kept a safe distance from him.

Slowly opening the door, Winston saw the gunman standing toward the middle of the customer lounge. He grinned at Winston, "I reckon you're thirsty," he said pointing to a used jelly jar filled with water on the coffee table. He offered Winston a seat near the coffee table while he sat on the opposite side cradling his shotgun in his lap. The gunman watched closely as Winston drank down the water.

"Listen," said Winston. "I have some goodies in my truck that you may have if you just let me go."

"What kind of goodies?"

"Household items including food and candy!"

"Candy you say?" The gunman rubbed his chin in thought, "Well, that's all well and good, but you see that's all mine anyway – including the truck."

The gunman's face went blank as if he lost interest and was getting bored by Winston's plea to release him. "I got a family waiting on me. Just let me go. You can keep the truck and everything in it, just let mah, please sir, let me gawwhow ...."

Winston felt his face sag, his jaw-dropping and his mouth wide open. He closed his mouth once, but he lacked the power to keep his jaw from sagging down. He began to hear his heart pounding in his head, and suddenly he realized he had to remind himself to breathe. Winston knew he'd been poisoned by something the gunman put in his water.

He struggled to put the words together as he slumped in his chair. The words the gunman was saying to him from across the table was something about the idea he wasn't going to feel any pain. "You see, I dropped some LSD in your water," came the voice laughing. "You'll be on an acid trip while Rustler takes you apart bit by bit, and you won't even care!

So take a look at Rustler standing out there foaming at the mouth. He's about ready to come in, and when I do let him in, he'll know it's dinner time!"

Much of what the gunman was saying came through loud and clear to Winston. It was just the way colors distorted and ran making the gunman's face look saggy like a bloodhound and the windows of this place heaved back and forth. It just wasn't right, and Winston struggled to escape the bonds of the LSD he had been given. He felt he was lying on the floor yet he wasn't. He was still where he was before, in a chair and however in two places at once. Soon he believed he was asleep and yet maybe dreaming that he was awake when he saw the gunman by the door. *How did he get there so fast?*

In a long blink of an eye, the gunman and Rustler were together inside the customer's lounge, and Rustler was standing erect next to the gunman. Winston never noticed how tall Rustler was; taller than the gunman as the two danced along the floor together. It was in no particular pattern the two danced and fell, bounced and fell ....

AFTERMATH

CHAPTER 6

Winston found himself lying on the floor. The heartbeat in his head still remained, but he had come back with his wits about him, and as far as he could tell he had escaped the hell of the acid trip he was on.

As everything began to come back into focus, he saw the gunman lying face up on the floor near the door. He was very still, and as Winston lied there, he stared at him, waiting to see him breathe. Winston's eyes rolled about looking for the shotgun. When he saw it, he knew the gunman was dead. The gunman was never without the reach of it and now also seeing the black form in the morning shadow, lie Rustler curled in the corner. Winston noticed something.

Rustler was not asleep.

How long Rustler had been staring at Winston he did not know. However, he did know by glancing slowly over to the scattered remains of the gunman that Rustler had eaten the better half of him. It was an odd thing that a sight such as this brought about a facsimile akin to that of when the scarecrow had been scattered by flying monkeys in the movie the Wizard of Oz came to mind.

Winston swallowed hard as he had a life or death decision to make. Getting to the door before Rustler was obviously impossible. However, jumping up and going for the parts room was the better decision. He had a clear shot from where he was, but it would be a draw. *If I can clear that counter to the other side before he tags me, I'm home free!*

Winston knew there was an exit door in the back of the parts room that led outside to the service bay area and where he parked his truck. He raised his head from the floor, and when he did, he noticed Rustler untuck his leg out from under him, ready to scramble after Winston. Slowly Winston lowered his head back to the floor, and as he did, he noticed Rustler relax slightly.

Easy now, he thought as he exercised his lungs slowly taking in large volumes of air and slowly exhaling. *On three ... one ... two ...*

Seconds later Winston hit the floor on the opposite side of the parts counter when he thought he heard himself say 'Three.' He liked being punctual. Pulling together a running stance he raced for the far wall of the parts room and searched for the door as he turned right along the wall. Overhead, he saw the 'Exit' sign, but he saw no door!

He looked up at the 'Exit' sign and saw the upper part of the door frame. The rest of the door was blocked by a large steel Vidmar ™ Cabinet. Winston tugged and shoved frantically trying to get the cabinet to move. He stopped to look around. There had to be something in this parts room he could use to pry the Vidmar ™ away from the door enough to gain access to the push-bar to let him escape this place. The only thing he could get his hands on in a hurry was a broom nearby, and he grabbed it with the idea that if he could gain access to the push-bar, he might get the door open and then climb over the top of the cabinet and get free.

He heard Rustler's toenails clicking on the concrete just a few aisles over. *Change of plan*, he thought as he clamored to get on top of the Vidmar ™ Cabinet, broom in hand.

Being trapped on top of the cabinet had its redeeming qualities in such that there was enough space above the cabinet and the top of the exit door that could accommodate his escape. That is if he could reach down between the cabinet and the door frame with the broom handle and push back the door release bar. Once the door was opened, Winston knew he could then drop down from the cabinet and escape through the door.

Rustler soon found Winston and took a seat at the Vidmar ™ and patiently watched as Winston tried to reach the push-bar to release the door and swing it open. After what seemed an eternity of struggling, Winston noticed the door had been welded shut. His heart sank as he looked down to Rustler whose dark and curious eyes looked back waiting for Winston's next move. The idea to swat at Rustler with a broomstick seemed like a stupid move, so instead, Winston grabbed a small white box from an adjacent shelf and dug out a water pump. Throwing the water pump down the aisle with all his might, Rustler jumped up and ran to go fetch it. Winston immediately took off for the parts counter and pushed through the exit doors from the customer's lounge.

There wasn't much time to think, but react instead, so when Winston pushed through the door leading outside to safety, he breathed a sigh of relief. He turned to look across the service lane to his truck and wondered if he should take the time to go ahead and load up his tools and fuel extender. As he stood thinking over the idea, he heard something drop by his feet. *Dammit*, in the dark oaths he swore, *it's a water pump!*

Surprised now, not because he saw Rustler sitting at his feet, as now he realized the dog could push through the customer lounge doors, just as he had moments ago.

AFTERMATH

Another thing he'd never seen was Rustler wagging his tail! Winston wasn't sure how long that happiness would last, so he forced a casual stride toward his truck. Reaching the gate, he unlocked the padlock and swung the gate open, returning to his truck to find Rustler once again, dropping the water pump at his feet.

"Okay boy," sighed Winston. "Go fetch."

This time he put a lot more distance on the water pump, and it touched down on the concrete service lane and rolled then skid the length of three lift bays. Rustler was down and then back with his new fetch toy by the time Winston was pulling the gate closed. He was preparing to padlock the gate down all the while they each stared back at one another. He was leaving behind a dog to wander alone in a death camp where Rustler would slowly die in agony. Even after what he went through, he wasn't sure he could handle leaving him to that horror.

"Now I know according to your previous owner, you have never been in the wild or outside this place, but I think you'll do alright."

Winston reopened the gate, but Rustler just sat there as if to say he wasn't allowed outside the fence. "Come on boy!"

Rustler stood and ambled out the gate to the truck. Winston secured the gate and returned to his vehicle and got in behind the wheel. Closing the door, he glanced over to Rustler and told him 'Good Luck!'

As Winston slowly backed out to the street, he saw Rustler lower down to rest in a prone position.

* * *

The sun was slowly setting when Winston took another trip around the block just to see if Rustler moved on, but he was still there. Rustler had a way of affecting your heart, but Winston knew the dog was young and pretty smart; he would do alright he figured.

Winston hit the open road for home. It had been a horrifying two days ... or was it three? He knew he was beyond the point of feeling hungry anymore. Even so, the thought crossed his mind a second time when in the diminishing light of the evening revealed a long shadowy form moving across the road in front of him. Winston reached behind his seat fingering the pump shotgun as he slowed down his truck and slowly pulled off onto the side of the road. He slid the shotgun to his lap and swung open the truck door and eased himself out. Fixing his sight on the long figure as it moved toward the tall grass beyond the roadside ditch, was the largest alligator Winston had ever seen. The tail alone was twice as long as Winston, and when he came close, the beast flung back his head and bellowed out a loud warning that ended in a hiss. Out of instinct, Winston leaped back. An encounter of this kind could easily end badly for him he knew, but the payoff could determine the difference between his family going to bed hungry or waking up tomorrow with the strength to move forward.

Many times in the past Winston visualized opening up the garden to a full half acre and adding the last of those Non-GMO corn seeds grow in abundance. He needed to build more drying bins for his excess corn crop for seed stock. He and his family can't-do all that on an empty stomach, he thought while staring down at the big gator.

Winston moved in closer, crossing the ditch trying to get a clean shot to the head of the alligator. Even with his shotgun loaded with slugs, he knew he needed to get close to the head of the animal to allow penetration. Though having a tough hide, there's a small crusty oval above and to the rear of the eye of a gator where the leather was thinnest and thus the target spot for Winston's shot. This spot represented the area of the temple on this beast where just one shot is all that was needed to kill it.

Steading his shotgun Winston pulled the trigger and immediately jumped backward. The colossal beast lurched up and rolled through the grass; again and again, it rolled while Winston moved safely back from the thrashing alligator. In all the many times Winston had killed alligators, this he knew, was a case of the creature nerves firing away after death. It was only the nerves firing off a series of chain reactions that triggered such violent defensive muscle contractions. It would be an hour before he could approach the alligator and attempt to handle it.

Sitting now on the tailgate of his pickup truck, an idea popped into Winston's head to mark the area and head back to see if Rustler was still sitting by the gate. It was about a half hour to go back and then with the return, here again, would be an ideal way to pass the time without having to hassle with the mosquitoes. He also needed an excuse to relieve his conscience of abandoning Rustler; just to know he took off and is making it on his own.

Pulling an old shovel and a tattered white tee-shirt from the back of his pickup truck Winston stuck the shovel in the ground and tied the shirt to the handle making it into a makeshift flag marking the location of the alligator. He then climbed back into his truck and headed back to the dealership.

AFTERMATH

CHAPTER 7

On the drive back to the dealership service gate, Winston thought about that alligator. Since there would be no way of loading it into the back of the truck in one piece, he would have to spend about an hour butchering the alligator on the side of the road and taking only the prime cuts home. Still, that would be at least 80 to 100 pounds of clean white meat. The rest of the gator would be worthless hide, bone, and cartilage anyway.

The pickup truck headlights swept across the service entrance gate as Winston circled around to stop next to the chain-link fence near the place he last saw Rustler. He felt a tinge of sadness shadow over him at seeing the dog had left. There was something about Rustler that Winston saw in the big dog's eyes; a gentle soul perhaps. Rustler had been an abused dog, who had never seen a loving hand, only a kick, punch or a mean word thrown his way. It was no wonder to Winston the chance he saw when the gunman dropped his guard and Rustler attacked him. Perhaps Rustler saw good in Winston when he offered him food and candy and a gentle pat on the head.

Winston sighed as he stopped the truck and shoved the stick gear selector stick into the 'Park' park position and shut off the engine. It was difficult for him to forget Rustler and he couldn't pin down the reason in his mind why that was. He began to realize that Rustler saved his life. It was an example of life perhaps which, heaven can move in inexplicable ways. Winston felt fortunate in that he was alive because of Rustler. Maybe it was now, feeling safe and secure in the thought that while he was here, he could retrieve his tools and fuel extender. Winston grabbed his flashlight from the car charger in his truck and walked over to open the gate, and while doing so, he felt the presence of someone tapping him on the shoulder with a baseball bat.

Standing behind him was a lone stranger, heavily tattooed and ugly as a boar hog on steroids. "Give me the keys to your truck, or I'll make a home run out of your head!"

The bandit made one mistake, and that was pushing Winston in the stomach with the ball bat. Over and over he jabbed at Winston, pushing him against the fence until Winston struck back at the bandit grabbing his bat engaging him in a tug of war and a struggle for possession. However, Winston was no match for this big guy's strength, and while he attempted to charge head-on into the bandit's stomach, he was instead lifted off his feet and body slammed on the ground; the ball bat clattering off to one side. Winston made an effort to raise himself from the ground, his lungs utterly void of air from the shock of being slammed to the ground, felt the ball bat slam against his upper back and shoulders. Winston was jarred by the shock of the ball bat striking him that he fell prone to the ground and as if a cork had popped free of his throat, air once again filled his lungs.

Winston's recovery from being body-slammed was about to be short-lived as the bandit straddled him from behind and yanked his head back exposing his throat. The bandit being larger than Winston and much stronger, "You should have listened to me the first time," the bandit said brandishing a knife in Winston's face. "I would have let you live."

Having all his weight on his neck made it impossible for him to fight from having his throat sliced open.

Out of the darkness came Rustler leaping through the air hitting the bandit with such a force that sent him flying into the fence. The bandit struggled to wrestle himself free from Rustler's jaws on his shoulder and neck, that he screamed to Winston to help him.

Winston got up and yelled to Rustler to stop. Surprisingly, Rustler heeled and backed away. They both stood a moment seeing the terror in the bandit's eyes and his shirt rip away and hanging around his waist while a rivulet of blood ran down across his bare chest. "You're lucky he isn't hungry, or I wouldn't have been able to stop him," said Winston as he reached over and scratched Rustler behind his ears. "Good boy, yeah you're a good boy."

"This ain't over," sobbed the bandit. "I'm coming back later with a gun!"

"Oh, now that's brilliant," Winston replied with a chuckle. "Yeah, you come back later when Rustler here is good and hungry."

The bandit stood and then skirted around Winston and Rustler a safe distance away before breaking into a full run into the night. Winston was still quivering from the excitement of almost being killed for the second time in three days. Rustler seemed to sense that and followed behind Winston as he made his way over to his truck. Pulling the basket of goodies from the passenger side of his vehicle, Winston set it down in front of Rustler. A few pounds of salted pork and a fistful of cane sugar and molasses candy disappeared by the time Winston returned from the machine shop with his tools and a case of fuel treatment and extender. After loading up his stuff in the back of the truck, he relocked the gate, knowing that he'd be back to collect his other set of tools in the lift bay.

* * *

AFTERMATH

A friendship bond had been forged that evening, and Winston was becoming more and more amazed at Rustler's intelligence. Rustler enjoyed being handled and ruffed up a bit by Winston's playful jostling of his head and ears.

When it was time to leave, Winston paused by the door of his pickup truck. It was by the grace of heaven above that he made it alive tonight. And as Rustler nudged him, Winston looked down to his friend who was looking back at him with sad eyes as if to say, he was sent to protect him too.

"Get in," Winston said while holding the door of his truck open for Rustler.

Never hesitating, Rustler jumped in as if he was an old time traveler heading off to parts unknown. "We're heading home, but first we got a chore to take care of."

Rustler was a little fidgety and couldn't hold back his excitement at hearing the motor startup. "Easy big boy. Easy, just relax."

Winston made the turn on to the highway and gently picked up speed. Rustler immediately did what any dog does, and hung his head out the window.

Winston drove along keeping a sharp eye out for his roadside marker, and when he came to the spot, he pulled off the road and parked with his headlights aimed at the lifeless body of the alligator. Rustler was quick to follow Winston, excited now and dancing around, sniffing in the tall grass until coming to the alligator carcass. Winston smiled. "Betchya haven't seen anything like that before."

Seeing Rustler latch his jaws on the tip of the gator's tail, Winston was surprised to see the dog twisting and yanking hard until he had dragged the half-ton alligator up from the ditch. Turning away with a smile and a shake of his head, Winston reached down into the bed of his truck and retrieved his pruning saw and his favorite hunting knife and tossed them in a five-gallon bucket.

Winston immediately went to work cutting free the two large jowls from the corner edges of the alligator's mouth and tossing both chunks of white meat into the bucket. Rustler worked on the other end, content to chewing away the tip of the tail. He then took the saw and cut off an alligator hand and tossed it to Rustler as a tasty doggy chew. With the saw in hand, Winston sawed the tail free of the gator and dragged it over to his pickup truck and wrestled it into the bed of the truck. Using his tailgate as a butcher block, he slit the hide from one end to the other and peeled the meat free of the leather. Running his hunting knife down the length of the tail, he separated all four cores of meat from the cartilage that ran the length of the tail. Tossing away the long strips of cartilage, he repacked the meat back inside the tail hide and tied the hide closed with some short lengths of twine.

"Come on Rustler, let's go!"

Rustler jumped back into the truck and took his place nearest the passenger window. Winston pulled the truck back out on the highway and headed home.

CHAPTER 8

~Joseph~

Joseph stood in the darkness. No lamps were burning – no lights whatsoever. The entire house was dark, and from where he stood in the doorway between the kitchen and living room, he waited for the sound he heard growing louder and louder to reveal itself where he could see it. In the faint light of a moon casting light on the porch outside, Joseph watched as the dim light flicker briefly shedding light through the doorway and across the floor of the living room. As the light swept by, the sound of his father's pickup truck approaching the house lifted Joseph's heart.

With the sound of the truck door slamming, Joseph noticed the dark form of a large animal dash by the porch. He could hear the footfalls of the racing animal as it disappeared out of sight and around the house. Circling the house entirely, the animal continued again never stopping to slow down. Then suddenly, he heard the voice of his father call out the name 'Rustler.'

It was a dog? A huge one indeed and his father and the dog walked together toward the porch. Silhouetted in the moonlight, the two took a few steps up on the porch and stopped. "Dad?"

"Yes it's me," he answered, and then gave the order for the dog to sit on the porch in which, surprisingly, Rustler obeyed. As his father entered letting the screen door slam closed behind him, he asked his son where everyone was and why there were no lights in the house.

"I think everybody is gone."

Joseph saw the impact of his words on his father.

The look of shock fell over his father's face, "Joseph, what do you mean gone?"

Expecting a reply, Winston stumbled over something laying on the floor on his way to where a table lamp should be. He then fumbled with a matchstick striking it

AFTERMATH

under the table as he had done so many times in the past. The living room began to glow in warm yellow light from the lamp and there in the middle of the floor was a pair of woman's jeans. A shoe was in the corner of the room as if cast aside or thrown at something or someone. Winston picked up the table lamp and walked over to his bedroom, and then the pantry looking, searching, and calling out his wife's name; and daughter's too. There was no one except his son in the house who stood speechless and wide-eyed.

* * *

Winston:

"Joseph, tell me what happened here," said Winston taking the rifle from the shaking hands of his son.

"They came, and I heard – they came, bad men, they came!"

Despite feeling his heart beginning to pound in his chest, Winston tried to calm his son. "Joseph, stop. Just take a deep breath and tell me from the beginning what went on here – from the beginning okay?"

Joseph swallowed hard and began to recall everything from the beginning when he was behind the house in the garden pulling up radishes and peas to snack on. He told him about seeing two men come into the house and his mother and sister screaming. He then went on about how he ran away and hid in the forest across from the house, waiting for his chance to sneak into his room and get the rifle that he had hidden under his bed.

Joseph stared at the floor, and then looked up to his father. "When it turned dark, I snuck through my bedroom window, got the rifle and that's when you came home."

"Did you see what they were driving and which way they left?"

"I don't think they had a car," Joseph replied shrugging his shoulders. "They must have left before dark, and they must have gone out the back door of the house because I didn't see them or mom and Darby.

Winston rubbed his chin. Ten acres behind his small farm was the Hartley access road that led to a truck farm to the east and Tamiami Trail to the west. He guessed that the kidnappers snuck up from a vehicle they had parked on the Hartley access road. That stretch of road was directly in front of the Fisher's ranch house. Pete Fisher was always attending to chores around his place, Winston knew. Maybe he had seen something.

Winston asked Joseph to sit down on the sofa. Holding the gun in one hand, Winston swung the door open to the porch and invited Rustler inside. Rustler got up and trotted into the house. Winston held a steady eye on the dog as he went right up to Joseph wagging his tail. Joseph's eyes widened with a smile, "He's ours?"

"Yes, and he loves to have his ears gently scratched."

Joseph and Rustler took to each other as if they had been lifelong friends as Winston told him how the dog had saved his life twice while out on the road and how he helped field dress one of the largest alligators in Florida! And since neither of them could sleep Winston, Rustler, and Joseph went outside to the truck to bring in the gator meat. Winston loaded some oak wood in the smoker and sliced up the gator tail into two inch thick steaks and then tossed them into a pot of boiling citrus water to marinade for ten minutes while the smoker got ready. Joseph took his dad's rechargeable flashlight out to the garden and pulled up some potatoes, cut some corn and some snap beans. Apparently, it was Rustler's first encounter with vegetables and took a cob of corn and a fistful of snaps and chowed-down on them like it was his last dinner. They hadn't loaded the smoker until the gator meat had a chance to cool. Joseph snuck a whole gator jowl to give to Rustler, and the entire three pounds of meat disappeared with Rustler running out to the porch to relax and enjoy his meal.

Joseph pitched in, helping his father gear-up to hit the road and search for Darby and his mom. It became evident to the boy to wonder if his father might be setting him up to have a couple of dinners put away for him while his father was away. "I guess you and Rustler are going out looking for mom and Darby while I stay home?"

Winston looked over his shoulder briefly as he was loading the meat into the smoker. "What gave you that idea?"

Joseph hated to be left alone at home, especially when there might be some evil men lurking about somewhere. "Then you mean I'm going?"

"Of course."

"And Rustler too?"

"Look, Joseph," Winston began. "We're taking a few days' provisions with us and whatever else we need." Winston's brow furled, pausing a moment to swallow. "We're bringing your mom and sister home!

Now if you can do me a favor and get everything out of the back of the truck except the fuel can and ammo box, I'd appreciate it. I'll fetch my tool chest because it's a little too heavy for you okay?"

Winston turned and grabbed up his son and hugged him. It was a long hug, and Joseph felt his dad sigh. He also saw the moonlight glisten in the glassy eyes of his father and knew for the better half of him that he too had to remain strong. They felt a nudge from the nose of Rustler who came up, and it put a smile on the face of Winston and his son who then said, "Dad, I think he wants a hug too."

AFTERMATH

Clearing his throat, Winston said, "We'll give the meat a few hours to smoke. It will hold its moisture and freshness wrapped tightly in banana leaves for a few days in the dry cooler."

* * *

Winston arose at the break of dawn and shuffled out of his bedroom with having only slept a few hours' sleep to maintain the day's activities that lay ahead. He saw Rustler and Joseph curled up on the bed still fast asleep. There was still plenty to do, and little time to get it done, so while a moment was taken to freshen up in the kitchen sink, Winston splashed water on his face and smoothed out his black hair with a hairbrush his wife kept on the bed stand next to her side of the bed.

Stepping outside, the mornings gentle breezed felt cool on his face. His eyes moved toward the shed where his smoker sat. Gone now was the billowing smoke from the smoker. It had wound down to just a faint remnant of smoke trailing out of the smokestack. Nearby, between the shed and a large stand of bananas was a picnic table where he could set up and wrap the jowl and tail steaks. Cutting two long 6 foot by 3-foot broad banana leaves, Winston spread them down on the picnic table. Checking the gator meat, Winston opened the smoker and removed the first batch of smoked meat. Winston was pleased to see the meat. It had a beautiful patina of gold and brown, and with the salt, he chipped off an old deer lick and pounded into fine granules, he salted down each chunk of meat before wrapping it tightly in the banana leaf.

Winston looked up after hearing the galloping footfalls of Rustler's paws hitting the ground. Rustler only stopped briefly, curious to see what Winston was doing. No doubt the euphonious scent of the smoked gator meat woke him up; however, it was not enough to quell his curiosity to stay long. Rustler had his sights on exploring and ran off to the woods across the road. Winston smiled; *Rustler was enjoying for the first time in his life what a dog loves to do ... explore the forests!*

While Winston was busy loading the truck with a dry cooler filled with smoked gator meat, Joseph joined him and dumped a few dozen red potatoes in the back of the truck. Corn, field peas, tomato, carrots, and a few radishes were added to the mix while Winston loaded several split oak logs bundled together with twine.

"Better throw a log on the fire," Winston told his son. "Yonder comes to breakfast!"

Joseph glanced out across the way to see Rustler, a wild piglet hanging limply in his jaws. "Run and get the rifle Joseph – quickly boy!"

The piglet's mother was on to Rustler, and after following him out of the woods, she took off after him like a runaway freight train. Rustler sensed the situation had turned against him and he took off running with the piglet in his mouth.

Winston could see there was no other way around shooting the piglet's mother as it was apparent the piglet was already dead. Also real was the fact that a wild hog as big as this female could easily gore and kill a dog. In most cases, a wild boar was fearful of humans, but in this case, things may be different. Winston had already pulled his shotgun out of his truck and was ready, hoping for the moment he wouldn't have to shoot the hog. He didn't want to piss it off or scare it off with an injury that would cause pain and suffering. However, the last he checked, he had six rounds left in the shotgun magazine, and that would be enough to kill the beast.

Then something unexpected happened. Before Rustler got close to Winston, he dropped the piglet and whirled around to face the mother hog. Rustler was ready to take on the beast, his ears straight up and the hair along his back stood up like a Mohawk. The mother hog stopped and tried to maneuver around to get a clear shot at goring Rustler in the ribcage, she grunted loudly as Rustler darted for a chance at latching on to her neck.

The sound of the rifle racking the slide made Winston look beside him at Joseph. The boy took aim at the hog and fired off a round that struck the wild boar in the head. The hog's forelegs suddenly gave out, and the hog fell to her side immediately. Joseph had shot the hog squarely between the eyes.

The shot took the hog down as a distance of about 45 feet away. They each grabbed a foreleg and dragged the wild boar over the shed. "I take it you've been practicing with the rifle."

Joseph just smiled nodding his head saying, "Not really. Just shooting the way you taught me."

Winston felt a sense of pride; his son was growing up to be a fine young man. He remembered his father telling him of the old Indian ways, that a boy was ready to become a man at the age of 12. Maybe at the age of 10, he was already there.

AFTERMATH

CHAPTER 9

Getting ready to search for the rest of his family helped to go a long way into keeping their minds busy and away from the nightmare of what had happened. It was the intense focus of dressing out the piglet, and its mother, and restocking the smoker with a load of split oak that kept them going. Once all that was done, Winston, Joseph, and Rustler left the smoker to do its job while they loaded themselves into the truck and headed out through the back acre of Winston's homestead for Hartley Road.

It had been a long time since Winston traveled this road and he was surprised to see how overgrown with tall grass Hartley Road had become. Winston stopped the truck. Tire tracks leading off the shoulder of the road ended where a vehicle had stopped near the end of where a bay-head of sugar cane ended, and cornrows began. Where the vehicle had stopped and where it resumed was evident in the large divot left in the ground where the driver had turned sharply and gunned the engine to pull away from the soft soil beneath the grass. Winston jumped out of the truck, as did Joseph and Rustler. Following behind Winston Rustler sniffed along the tracks as if he were Bloodhound and not a Rottweiler. Noticing Rustler's interest in tracking, Joseph told his dad that maybe they should bring along something belonging to his mom and Darby.

Winston looked at Rustler's body language and smiled knowingly at his son, "Maybe so ... maybe so."

They both followed Rustler out to the road where the tracks had made a U-turn heading west toward Tamiami Trail. A man waving his arms attracted Winston's attention. He was a white-haired gentleman dressed in denim overalls and wearing an old straw cowboy hat. Winston knew the man whose name was Pete Fisher, and he lived across the road in an old ranch house. Pete and his two sons operated a cattle ranch which is why it was hard to trade fresh meat for fresh vegetables at the truck farm. Winston had in the past traded truck repair work for some of the fruits and vegetables he did not grow himself.

"Hey Winston," said Pete Fisher. "Sorry about the damage to your cornfield."

Winston had been too busy to notice. "That's alright Pete ... cows got loose again?"

"Sure did. Ronnie and Carl rounded her up yesterday afternoon after a car swung out of control and punched a hole in my fence."

Winston's eyebrows raised and frowning he asked, "When exactly did that happen?"

"Around 3 or 4 'o clock yesterday afternoon."

"Did you talk to the driver?"

"No, sir. They struck that post over there, then backed up and hauled-ass toward the main highway."

The old man followed Winston as he crossed the road over to the broken fence post. He could see the new post had been put in its place with the old broken one still lying in the tall grass. A white paint streak marked the post. "What color was the vehicle Pete?"

Pete rubbed his chin, "It was white, but it had all kinds of spray-painted graffiti on it."

"What kind of graffiti?"

"I don't know," Pete began. Looking down he plucked a weed to chew on and thought awhile. "You know, I think the one word that sticks in my mind is the word MOOSE. I believe I saw that car down at the truck farm awhile back. There were two men, and they were giving the truck farm owner trouble. Something about wanting free samples. Can you beat that?"

"So what happened?"

"The owner just gave them watermelon and cantaloupe and told them to get off his farm and not come back. They threatened him and then left."

Winston tilted his head and stared at Pete as if waiting for more information. "Well, what kind of threat did they make?"

Pete swayed with indignation, "The idiot and his big friend told them that they'd come back when everyone was asleep and kill them!"

Winston ran his fingers through his hair, and his eyes narrowed, "There were two men right?"

"Yes."

"And how many did you see yesterday. I mean when you saw the car smack into your fence post over there."

Pete said almost immediately, "Three or four—three for sure."

Everything seemed to fit. The story Joseph son told him about the two men and the fact that they showed up seemingly out of nowhere. There weren't many cars out there that ran; however, also, if the men turned on to Tamiami Trail, it would be a toss of the coin as to which direction they went. There was the business district of Hartley between here and Tamiami Trail less than 5 miles up the road. The last time

AFTERMATH

Winston was up that way, he saw most of the town was shut down or abandoned. That is most if not all the businesses were empty including the police department. Homes remotely located in Hartley were modest and sat on large parcels of land. Winston knew he could do a drive-by check of all the houses in the area in less than one afternoon. Sooner or later Winston knew he would find these men, but first, before heading over to the truck farm, he needed to check on the progress of the smoker and grab a few things.

* * *

About an hour of packing meat, and gathering some clothing left on the floor of the living room area, Winston and his son were ready with Rustler to go visit the truck farm. Winston was hoping to find out if the men had been customers of the truck farm and had visited on more occasions other than the one Pete Fisher spoke of.

This time, after reaching the ranch home of the truck farm owner, Winston honked the horn on his truck as instructed by the sign out front. The owner came out toting a shotgun as seemed the protocol these days.

"You here for produce?" asked the slim old gentleman.

Winston noticed the swollen knuckles of the man's hand holding the rifle slung over one shoulder. He had severe arthritis and walked with a limp and Winston remembered him when he was in better shape before all the hard work caught up with him.

He studied Winston's face then broke into a toothless smile, "Why you're the mechanic feller!"

"Yes sir and that's my son Joseph and sitting in the back is my dog Rustler."

He gave a tilt of his head, and then asked, "You couldn't have shown up at a better time. My crop sprayer runs, but cuts out every 5 or ten minutes or so – but starts right back up easy enough."

Winston told him he'd look at it some other time. "I have reason to believe the two guys who threatened to kill you and your family kidnapped my wife and daughter."

"You don't say. They'd a dunnit for sure."

"Did those guys come around to your farm before the time they made their threats?"

"They came a time or two, mostly wanting to trade using jewelry, books and other stuff I assume was stolen. Then the last time they showed up with nothing to trade with but threats. They started shoving me around, so I gave them a few melons and a trunk-load of citrus and told them never to come back. That's when they made their threats. Haven't seen them in a few days."

"Could you describe them?"

"One was skinny and cocky, the other ugly and fat."

"Anything about the car you could tell me?"

"It was about a 1977 Olds Cutlass Supreme. White with a bunch of messed up writing on it."

"MOOSE?"

"Yeah, that was one of the things painted on it."

The conversation halted abruptly as the old man began to stare-off in the distance behind the truck. His voice seemed to come from a faraway place, "Folks try to mix gas with other things like kerosene, diesel and maybe oil just to keep their 'ol cars running."

"Trust me," Winston said. "That ain't a good idea."

The old farmer raised his bony old hand and pointed toward the road. "I remember now, that Oldsmobile burned oil and smoked like a mosquito fogger."

Winston turned his head to look behind him at the road. A good distance away, Winston saw a dirty white car pull out across the road; a white cloud of smoke pouring out the exhaust.

Winston quickly fired up his truck and told the old man he was grateful for his help and promised to drop by and look at his crop sprayer soon as he spun his truck around and headed down the road for the Oldsmobile. "Hang on Joseph, we're going to get your mother and sister back!"

CHAPTER 10

~Dug and his brother Justin~

Justin outweighed his brother Dug by two-to-one, which is why Dug did all the driving. Justin hated driving, as did Dug, however, Dug always did what his big fat brother wanted. Both men considered themselves outlaws, and in the romantic sense; legends in their own time.

Most of Justin and Dug's day was spent robbing and trading goods for other useful products. Some things were easy 'pickens,' others not. Midnight raids on gardens like Winston Sawyers farm were easy. A bushel of corn, some peppers and carrots might never be missed, but things like raiding prepper's bunkers for stored meals weren't. Preppers seemed to have a network of other prepper friends and would gladly hand out the information on where to find those bunkers, just to keep from being shot. So Justin kept a list of those locations and anyone giving out false information was always repaid a visit and burned out of their bunkers or lined up and shot. After all being lawless was easy these days; however, the competition in their field of business was fierce. Breaking in on the 'high-end,' of smuggling humans was an art-form, and very lucrative in the world of wealth-sharing. Justin, having learned of the aspects of trading and trafficking with the 5 families in Tampa had him excited about breaking free of this small time racket he was running. It was his first trade deal with the 5 families that opened his eyes to the wealth and lavish way of life that was springing up in Tampa. Justin wanted to get in on this way of life but had yet to develop an idea of how to go about it.

In Tampa, there are 5 oil refineries with each one run by a private family. These were the families of a culture set within the landscape of a dead and dying city. Most areas of the city that weren't abandoned were sparsely populated by desperate people who roamed the streets looking to survive any way they could. However, circling the 5 mansions of the rich and powerful, were private guards whose time was spent trapping down and tossing the bodies of those who had managed to enter the property by scaling the walls. Trafficker and suppliers under strict supervision were allowed to enter.

On their next trip to Tampa, Justin and Dug hoped to see a beautiful European car there, just for them as promised. Justin remembered seeing all the cargo ships and all the oil tankers heading in and out of Tampa Bay and wondered what other kinds of goods made up these families' business.

Justin pulled out a tattered notebook from the car's glove compartment. Pencil in hand, he began scribbling down a few ideas he wanted to ask when he and Dug would, at last, deliver that woman and her daughter to the Tampa Families. For the first time, he and his brother Dug had developed a plan. Never before had such an idea require such intense planning and time and involve so much thinking. Dug did most of the planning and thinking and with it all, the headaches to prove it.

Justin glanced over to Dug, "How do you spell marijuana?"

Dug didn't comment. He was busy looking up at his rear-view mirror at a pickup truck coming up behind them flashing their headlights. "We know anyone in a faded red pickup truck?"

A surprised expression on Justin's face quickly turned to a look of panic. Behind them was the pickup truck he and Dug so cleverly kept an eye on earlier. It was the truck belonging to the Sawyer farm they had raided. Four days earlier, the absence of the red pickup signaled to Justin and Dug that Winston was away. And after two days they were sure to make their move on the Sawyer Farm.

Now it appeared the truck was back and hot on their trail. "Dog-it Dug," cried Justin.

"We'll lose 'em!" Dug said while flooring the gas pedal.

Justin quickly grabbed his brother's knee in a counter-gesture, "No Dug – just act natural. We ain't no match for his truck."

The red pickup truck driven by Winston Sawyer roared up close behind Dug and Justin's beat up Olds Cutlass.

"He ain't passing us," said Dug; his head bobbing back and forth to the rear-view mirror. "He ain't even trying to pull us over or run us off the road."

Justin was checking his snub-nose .38 special and probing his pocket for a bullet to replace an empty round in the cylinder. Now loaded with all five rounds, Justin swung the cylinder to lock into place. Finally, he raised the pistol for Dug to see, "Just in case!"

"The shotgun, where's the damn shotgun?"

"Relax Dug, it's on the back seat, and it's loaded and ready."

Dug had heard about Winston and knew the man was a skilled hunter and would not hesitate to drag them off into the woods and kill them over what they'd done with his wife and daughter. Dug concealed his shaking hands by holding the steering wheel with both hands.

Justin instructed his brother not to go to the Laundromat like initially planned, but instead to allow Winston to follow them home. "When we get home, and he

AFTERMATH

jumps out of his truck holding a gun, we'll talk our way out of this. Otherwise if he gets out of his truck unarmed, I'll approach him like I was going to talk, but instead, I'll shoot him point blank in the forehead."

Apparently, it seemed like a good idea to Dug who laughed adding, "Sure Nuff. Could use a fine pickup truck like that."

"Yeah, I'm for that," said Justin snorting back a wad of snot. "A truck, all hopped-up and jacked-up like that one could fetch us a pile of trade goods."

Dug frowned. "I thought about that boat we saw by Howard Franklin's place. If we had us a fine pickup, we could hi-jinx that boat for ourselves. Maybe even catch us some fish."

"Oh yeah ... you know we could just hook up to that boat and pull her down to the lake and do just that!"

Of all the many times Justin had to save his brother Dug from drowning, it never made an impact on his brother's fear of the water. Dug loved wading out into the lake to cool off, but he never went farther than waist deep. And despite his many efforts to teach Dug to swim, he never caught on and would just go about drowning as usual. Sometimes while wading out, Dug would step into a hole and would commence drowning, so Justin always stayed close to his brother knowing he never learned to swim. In fact, Justin wondered how it was his brother learned anything. It took Dug a long time to learn to drive as Justin now recalled. The biggest problem with driving was learning the concept of the steering wheel and how that applied to the direction the vehicle would go. Before Dug got the hang of it, he'd go in the wrong direction a lot.

"Remember that canoe we stole a few years ago?"

Dug scratched his head and then grinned, "Oh yeah bro!"

"Remember the dumbass we stole it from?"

Dug laughed and shook his head, "Yeah, Wally Johnson. We weren't out no more than a few hundred feet from shore when that dumbass shot his own boat full of holes."

Justin smiled and swung back his head, "Luckily his aim was off or we'd a been kilt."

"Yeah, we'd a been dead all right! Instead, we damn near drowned."

"Speak for yourself."

Dug slapped his forehead, "Oh yeah, that's right you pulled me to shore by my hair!"

"Then what?"

"Oh uh?" Dug stammered trying to remember the rest of that day and the weeks to follow. "Yeah, well, old man Johnson made us work off the price of the boat since we didn't have the money to pay for a canoe that was laying on the bottom of a lake." Dug glanced over to his brother and snickered, "Yeah and you lost a hundred pounds working off the price of that boat!"

Justin just shook his head and pursed his lips. "And you know something?"

"Whaaa?"

"Somehow I believe it all went in his favor. What, with the price of the boat versus two weeks of hard labor digging and setting fence posts around a 40-acre field and all ... well, it just feels like he set us up to steal that canoe!"

"You mean just so he could get some free work done?"

Justin squirmed in his seat and hung his head low. "I do feel bad now about burning down his barn now that I think about it."

"So what? It was my idea, Justin."

"I know," Justin said breathing a heavy sigh. "Old man Johnson fed us pretty good that week or two, and besides, he could have killed us while we were in the canoe."

"Mmm, yeah, nobody's aim could be that far off."

AFTERMATH

CHAPTER 11

~Hartleytown Laundromat~

Mary Sawyer and her daughter Darby remained locked in the bathroom of one of many abandoned downtown buildings in the small town of Hartley. The sign out front simply read: Hartleytown Laundromat & Dry Cleaning.

Little Darby stood by the tiny window watching her mother's attempt at escaping to the outside. The window matching the size of a missing concrete block in the wall held very little promise of her escape. Mary was only able to squeeze her head and one shoulder past the opening of the bathroom window.

Mary, having previously counted her blessings, was able to free herself and little Darby from the twine used to bind their hands together. Their mouths were gagged with dirty socks found in a washing machine by the two kidnappers earlier yesterday afternoon. Shortly after freeing themselves, they found some relief from parched throats in the water found in a toilet flush tank. It made little sense to Mary why being gagged in a town where there was no one around to hear you screaming, was necessary. Also, the reason for being kidnapped in the first place made no sense to her. But then, Mary didn't spend much time thinking about that since her mind was more occupied with finding a way out of this place.

Whatever the misfortune that would become them, Mary could not bear to think of seeing her baby girl a victim of such. It had now become evident that she could not escape this bathroom with her daughter. Better her daughter escape alone than to face what evil was awaiting them soon. Mary blinked away the tears and drew a deep breath, and again, drew her daughter close, hugging her tightly while trying to find the words that she had to say to her.

Clutching her little girl's shoulders, Mary held Darby before her, face to face and told her to pay attention to every word she had to say. "I'm sending you on an errand," she said trying at best to hold a smile. "I'm sending you to the church to find the Preacher Brother Jonas."

Darby's frown grew, and her chin began to quiver. "But momma ... maybe there'll be strangers out there."

"Now Darby, I told you many times what to do if you see a stranger?"

Darby nodded. "Yes, momma. I run as fast as I can to the nearest house."

"And then what?"

"I go inside and yell for help." Tears began to stream down Darby's cheeks as she pointed to the small window. "But momma I wish you could come."

Again Mary hugged Darby as she explained in the way her 5-year-old could understand. "I know honey, but I can't fit through that window, but you can. And you're the best chance we've got to get Brother Jonas to help find your father."

Mary did not know what became of her husband Winston since he was long overdue to coming home. She feared he too was in trouble or dead. And her son Joseph was also missing, perhaps alone to fend for himself. A little comfort came to her in the thought that Joseph could take care of himself.

In contrast was Darby, a little girl barely 45 pounds and dressed like a little doll in a summer dress shivering and sobbing. "But momma I can't go," her voice squeaked.

Mary lowered her tone as she spoke, "You can, you will, and I don't mean maybe. You understand me?"

Darby nodded and turned to face the window. "Ye-Yes momma I'll go." And with that, Darby crawled through the window to the outside. Mary could hear little rubber flip-flops fade off in the distance.

Mary slowly sank to sit beside the small window; she covered her face in her hands and softly said, "Bye-bye baby, I love you."

* * *

Darby walked down to the corner of Main and Hastings Street not more than two blocks down from the Hartleytown Laundromat. It was a happy sight to see the church, and Darby skipped along to the stairway entrance and opened the door of the church and went inside. Brother Jonas was there, tapping away at some nails with a hammer when he looked up to see Darby smiling down on him. She recognized Brother Jonas from the many times she'd been to Sunday services. He was a large man but looked smaller when he was on his knees hammering on some nails that went into the floor holding down one of the benches that people would sit on during services.

He was such a wise man, she thought. *Oh, the way he looked over his gold-rimmed glasses and all!* He resembled Santa Claus, with his white hair and beard she mused to herself, feeling a bit shy, but knowing he really wasn't Santa Claus after all. He was just a preacher man that people was in awe of. And everyone wanted to shake his hand after services. *Every last one of them waited patiently to shake his hand!*

AFTERMATH

Like a man of his years, he labored to stand up, and when finally he did, he smiled and shook the dust from his knees, "Well well," he said jovially. "You are?"

Clasping her hands behind her back, she twisted shyly to and fro, "Darby."

"Darby," he responded, eyes turning up in thought. "Oh let me see now. You belong to the Sawyer family!"

"I sure do."

Brother Jonas sat down on the bench he'd been working on and looked face to face with little Darby. "So, young lady, what brings you to me?"

"Momma told me to get you to bring my daddy to the laundromat."

"So she did, did she?"

"Yup. I mean yes sir."

"And where shall we go to find your father?"

Darby's eyes opened wide as if to say she didn't know, and with a shrug of her shoulders, she said, "I don't know. Maybe he's at the house."

The preacher drew a serious expression, and for a short moment, he thought before asking, "And your mother? Where is she?"

Darby pointed in the direction, "She's at the laundromat."

The laundromat had been closed since the power went out over a year ago. There was no reason for Darby's mother to be there and that worried Brother Jonas. "Darby, why is your mother at the laundromat and not here with you?"

Little Darby just drew a deep breath, and with an exasperated tone she retorted, "She's in the bathroom and can't get out."

Brother Jonas picked up his carpenter hammer and said to Darby, "Oh we'll get her out, I promise you."

Not a minute later, Brother Jonas and Darby marched hand in hand to the Hartleytown Laundromat.

* * *

~Earlier~

Winston followed right in behind Dug and Justin as they pulled into the driveway leading up to their shack. He left his truck running while he got out and walked the short distance to come face to face with Justin. Seeing that Winston wasn't toting a gun, Justin fingered his .38 special in the pocket of his bib overalls and strained an eye on the dark figure sitting on the passenger side of the truck. There was a good chance he could shoot them both ... maybe. However, leaping out of the truck bed jumped Rustler.

"Sit boy," Winston told Rustler, and like a good dog, he did just that, right alongside his master.

Justin turned loose his pistol and let it nest back down to the bottom of his pocket. "What's up guy?"

Dug chimed in quickly asking, "Why is your dog crying and slobbering like that?"

"He likes you and the way you smell, and he's probably hungry," replied Winston.

A pause while Winston studied the expressions on the two brothers' faces.

Justin turned a glance to his brother Dug and then back to Winston. Justin then flashed a phony smile and said, "What?"

"My wife and child, where are they?"

Dug was the first to reply, "I don't know what you're talking about. And besides, this is private property."

Justin turned to his brother, "Shut-up Dug. Mister, if it'll make you feel better, you have my permission to check out the house, but you ain't gonna find your wife and kid in there."

Winston, without saying another word marched up to the house with Rustler following close behind him. Inside, Winston nearly gagged on the rotting odor of food and dirty dishes strewn about the front room. Household items like broken table lamps, magazines, and even bed springs littered the floor in tight groupings setting aside narrow walking trails from one room to the next. Rustler gracefully leaped over a broken end table for a paper sack of dog food he saw in the kitchen area.

There was the buzz of houseflies and the rustle of rat feet scampering through the mounds of trash, and while Winston turned back, satisfied his wife and daughter were nowhere about; he caught a glimpse of flumes of dry dog food raining down in the kitchen as Rustler slung the bag of dog food back and forth.

Rustler followed Winston out on to the front porch when the two men, Justin, and Dug came walking up. "Well mister," Dug said. "You satisfied?"

"What's your dog doing with our food?" asked Justin.

Glancing over to Rustler, Winston replied, "Your food? Ya'all don't have a dog."

Justin's face turned red when Dug spoke up, "How'd he know we done ate the dog months ago?"

"Shut up Dug. He didn't ask about eating no dog."

Winston paused not saying a word and then stepped off the porch for his truck. Rustler was there before him and jumped up, taking his bag of dog food and his place in the back of the truck.

Justin turned, belched a long burp and then whispered to his brother, "I feel like I'm the new owner of a 4X4 pickup truck today!"

Dug fanned the front of his face, "Dude, you got some bad breath."

"Yours smell like you ate a turd," Justin groaned while he wiggled his 38 special out of the pocket of his worn denim overalls.

AFTERMATH

    Backing out on to the road, Winston had swung the truck to the passenger side facing Dug and Justin. Winston was convinced these men had kidnapped his wife and daughter, but where they had them hidden was a mystery. Winston planned to camp out in the woods nearby where he and his son Joseph could keep watch over the men's activities. Justin and Dug would unknowingly lead him and Joseph to that place, he knew.

    Winston was already focused on a place where he and Joseph could set-up camp when suddenly the sounds of gunfire disrupted his thoughts. Shifting from reverse to forward, another shot rang out ending with a loud metallic clank. A bullet had hit the side door of the truck. Flooring the accelerator, Winston kicked up a mountain of dust in his path, when Joseph cried out to his father, he'd been shot.

CHAPTER 12

The sounds of glass crunching under Brother Jonas's shoes as he entered the Hartleytown Laundromat signaled to him that he'd better have Darby wait outside. The spongy rubber flip-flops she wore would only serve to collect embedded glass shards, so Darby found a place to sit on a bench outside the laundromat while she waited, confident in the thought that Brother Jonas would free momma from this place.

~Darby~

The sun was hot and not having shade to sit in, made daydreaming difficult for Darby, so she went directly across the street where there was a coin-operated 'flying pig' ride to sit on and plenty of shade.

Sitting in the saddle of the 'flying pig' a fantasy of daydreams filled her mind. She saw herself flying over the tree-tops to a place she had visited so many times with her family. It was a small lake daddy called, 'Gator Hole,' nestled within tall trees and it was a place where father would go to get fish for dinner. On Sundays, he would bring Joseph, and momma would set up a picnic lunch while she and her brother would paddle around in the lake. Darby was amazed at the amount of fish daddy would spear with his crossbow. Sunday dinner at home was always fish, mostly Nile Perch and yellow hominy or hushpuppies. Posole made with fish and peppers was also Darby's favorite, but momma only made that for dinner the day after or when it got too cold to go swimming.

Moments passed and somewhere between a daydream of picking lemons for momma's lemon custard pie and dressing her doll to go to church, Darby was jarred into the reality that those bad men had just come back to the laundromat.

The car's smoke still lingered in the air while both bad men exited the car. Standing in the doorway of the laundromat was Darby's mother and Brother Jonas.

Darby slid from the saddle of the 'flying pig,' and hid behind it. She crouched low keeping a watch on what was going on across the street through the forelegs of the pig. She heard shouting and saw her mother's eyes widen at the sight of the fatter of the two bad men draw a gun on Brother Jonas who was threatening the two with a claw hammer. Brother Jonas stepped in front of momma and rose up his hammer when the fat man shot him two times.

Darby wanted to scream but held a tight hand over her mouth instead. The thin man grabbed momma while the fat man tied her hands together. Tears welled up in Darby's eyes. It was happening all over again. Momma was pushed into the backseat of the car, and they sped off leaving Brother Jonas lying there in his own blood. Darby dashed across the street to Brother Jonas's side. She had never seen anyone dead before, but she knew he was dead because of the hole in his forehead. The angels would come to take him to heaven she knew. She stood up from Brother

AFTERMATH

Jonas's side and wiped away the tears. Those bad men had taken momma to another hiding place.

Hunger gripped her belly with the need to eat something, so Darby headed back to the church to see if she could find something to eat. As she walked along the storefronts of the many businesses, she tried to remember what they looked like before all the people went away. Many stores had their windows smashed while some just had the doors left wide open. They all seemed to take on a ghostly appearance. However, there was the Five and Dime, where she and momma had gone many times before. Darby forgot she was hungry and ventured inside; after all, the door was wide open just like it had been in the past. And although the store looked the same, almost all of the boring stuff was gone from the shelves. Except for the candy, but it too was gone. The rack had been tipped over and lying on the floor. Gingerly stepping around the rack of shelves, Darby caught a glimpse of something red and shiny on the floor beneath the shelving. She reached down and tugged the object free. It was a package of cherry licorice, and with it rolled out a cylinder-shaped roll of Necco Wafers ® candy. She smiled; she loved cherry shoestring licorice. Momma always said they couldn't afford such things as store-bought candy.

Darby's smile fell. Looking down at the candies in her hands, she decided to put them back where she found it. She didn't have any money and knew better not to take things that didn't belong to her. Taking things that didn't belong to you was stealing, she knew; unless a grownup said it was okay. But there weren't any grownups around, except for a portrait of a beautiful lady over the cosmetic counter. The lady seemed to be watching her, and her pretty eyes followed her as Darby moved about the store.

Over the time Darby spent shopping, she decided there was nothing that interested her. There was a small can wrapped in white paper that had a picture of a red devil dancing with a pitchfork in his hand. It scared Darby, and she dropped it on the floor. She then looked over to the portrait of the beautiful lady who seemed to suggest to her to stay a while longer. And then she remembered seeing Mrs. Michaels trying some free samples of perfume at the counter by the portrait. Darby, thinking about the time momma put lipstick on her lips, made her smile. She was attracted to the cosmetic counter as if pulled by an unseen force, curious to see if the lady in the portrait had run out of lipstick. But after making her way to the counter, she found the cosmetic bar empty and the glass lying inside the case in broken chunks. She noticed a metal top inside the case, and it was within reach. It was the kind of top that Darby was familiar with; the kind with the pull-up handle that would spin the top the faster you pumped the handle. Pictures of the circus were painted on it. Elephants, tigers, and clowns made up a scene in some faraway place that was happy, not sad.

Darby crouched down and sat on the floor with the top she had just found. A few pumps and the pretty top spun, the pictures blending into a circle of color, and something else; it played music! Darby pumped the handle over and over again, faster and faster, and the music picked up a tempo that was mesmerizing. Gazing at it now, she let the top wind down to where it began to wobble. Soon it tumbled on to its side, still spinning as it caught the traction to jog across the floor and bump into the lower baseboard of the cosmetic counter. Darby clapped her hands and laughed, for she had never had the chance to play with a toy such as this beautiful top. There was just so much this store had to offer, but the one thing she didn't expect to see was a shiny new quarter near where she fetched the top. As she studied the quarter in her hand, her eyes wandered to the place she had found it, and there it was, another coin; a penny and a nickel! She remembered a long time ago when her brother Joseph said to her after finding her doll's missing eyeball, "Finders keepers, and loser's weepers." Later that week, she recalled sneaking into his room and fetching her dolly's eye out of his cigar box of creepy things.

Grabbing up the three coins and the top, she dashed back over to where she had seen the roll of candy and the cherry licorice. At the store checkout counter, Darby placed the three items she wanted to buy. This was all so new to her; it was the things grownups did, and the first time she had purchased anything in a store. She knew the pretty lady in the portrait was watching her, so she said, "I wish to purchase these items, and here is the money!" Darby proudly set the coins on the counter and then bagged her items from a stack of bags lying on the floor.

Darby was proud of herself. She felt she was becoming a grownup as she strutted out the door of the Five and Dime.

* * *

~The Smoking Oldsmobile Breakdown~

An hour into their journey to Tampa, Dug and Justin's Oldsmobile blew a tire. Mary Sawyer never heard such foul language nor seen such displays of temper tantrums as that of Justin's brother Dug. The idea that they had no spare tire annoyed Justin to the point of blaming Dug for not replacing the spare tire that was once upon a time in the trunk.

"Just admit you're a dumbass," Justin shouted.

Dug countered the argument exclaiming, "You're the one that said forget about replacing it, in the first place!"

Justin drew a heavy sigh, "That's because we were going to pick up a brand new car in Tampa once we delivered the woman."

"So now we ain't," Dug shouted as he got out of the car and threw up his arms. "So what do we do now, fat ass?"

Justin got out of the car as Mary looked on from the backseat. Mary sent up a prayer to Saint Joseph and Annie Oakley. There was no time to work on the cord binding her hands behind her back, so to pull this one off, Mary had to stick her fanny out the rear window while guiding the shotgun between the cheeks of her buttocks and carefully look over her left shoulder.

Justin was busy yelling and poking his finger in Dug's face when Justin suddenly paused in mid-sentence. The scowl on Dug's face went flat, "What?"

Justin voice lowered, "Tell me you didn't leave the damn shotgun in the backseat."

"She's behind me with the shotgun right?"

"Yup," replied Justin, his eyes glazed in awe. "She does have a nice looking ass."

Mary let them have both barrels of the old 10 gauge. Having only fired a shotgun once before, she didn't realize that 10 gauge packed a bigger wallop than a mere 12 gauge. The kickback of the shotgun was like that of a mule. The buttstock of the rifle landed a blow under her lower jaw, driving her head into the car door.

Off in the distance, Mary heard birds and crickets chirping, and then there was darkness.

AFTERMATH

When Mary awoke it was beginning to get dark, and all was quiet. Her head pounded and her throat was dry. However, the only thing on her mind now was to release herself from the twine that was cutting into her wrists. She flipped herself around to her back and then sat up, almost surprised by the sound of the shotgun roll off her and landing on the floorboard with a thud; she now recalled what had transpired earlier. Struggling to a position to look out over the opposite door window, she saw the vermin she shot laying in the road. They had to be lying there for hours. Mary blew a sigh of relief and sent up a thank you to her benevolent heroes in heaven. Hopefully, now, she could tend to the business of getting back home again to her family. But first things first – the cord; get it free of her wrists.

Taking a position between the front two seats, Mary spied a bottle opener inside the recess in the console. Bracing herself, she flipped around facing the rear window and thrust her arms between the two seats with the hope of retrieving the bottle opener. As it turned out, it was an easy task as she grabbed up the bottle opener and then moved around to a more comfortable position. The bottle opener had an excellent handle on it, much like a utility knife she thought. But the best part was the can opener was part of the outer top side and represented the shape of a curved triangle. It slipped nicely between the bindings between her hands, and for the next half hour, Mary worked the bottle opener across the cord like the bow on a fiddle.

Once free, she tucked the bottle opener in the pocket of her dress and got out, re-entering the car from the front passenger side. There was very little light to see what was in the glove compartment, only the glow of a ¾ moon poking through the tree line from the western side of US Highway 41 Tamiami Trail. The shotgun in the backseat floorboards was a loathsome appliance, but Mary knew to make it home she needed protection, which meant she needed to find the ammunition for it. Thinking that she had searched everywhere, even the trunk, she began to wonder about the box of bullets she saw in the glove compartment. It was then she recalled the bigger of the two brothers had a silver-colored pistol he pulled out of his overalls and shot Brother Jonas. In a moment of thought, Mary reasoned that there were other desperate men about and that she would need that gun if she were ever to make it home safe. Mary went back around to the passenger side door and fetched up the box of bullets.

As she was heading around the other side of the vehicle to check Justin's pocket for the pistol, she noticed the figure of a man standing over the bodies. Mary froze in her tracks. The man never looked up as he knelt beside the two brothers.

"I take it you're the one who shot these two guys?"

Mary didn't say anything; she just turned and ran to the door and grabbed up the shotgun.

In the moments that passed, Mary had positioned herself around the trunk of the Oldsmobile. She held the shotgun on the man, watching as he slowly rose to his feet, still looking down. "Well looky here," he said softly, "this man had a gun. I guess you were justified in shooting them. Am I wrong?"

Mary's heart sank. Here was a stranger with a gun and unknown intentions and all she could think about is the box of bullets left on the passenger floorboard under the glove compartment.

She couldn't help shaking. "Yeah, I shot them. I'll shoot you too, so you better be on your way, mister!"

"Easy, easy," he replied. "Look, lady, I can see you have a flat tire, and some red-necks tried to take advantage of you, and you did what you had to do. I'm just saying, I'm here to help if you need me."

"You just drop that gun and go."

She couldn't make out his face, only that he seemed postured for taking a stand against her. Her heart banged against her ribcage, and she felt her face flush when he finally said, "Sorry ma'am I don't think I can do that."

"You'll do as I say or I'm shooting. Just take another step forward, and I'm going to shoot!"

Mary heard the stranger chuckle. "You know, I believe you will. I'm headed north and if you want to join up with me fine. Either way, I'm keeping this pistol."

She saw him tuck the pistol into his backpack as he turned and began walking away. Thinking back, she never thought of which direction this man had come up from and not trusting him she knew he chose to go north, which may not have been his destination at all. It was the indication that was apparently obvious in the direction of the Oldsmobile.

She watched the stranger disappear in the night, heading north in the opposite direction she was heading. Despite not knowing how far away she was from home, however just knowing all the while, it was the shotgun she held that kept her safe from being dragged away by this stranger.

Mary set the shotgun down, propping it against the side of the Oldsmobile and then headed south down Tamiami Trail.

AFTERMATH

CHAPTER 13

~Back at the Sawyer Homestead~

~Winston carried Joseph from the truck to the house~

Winston shouldered through the back door of his house, noticing as he did, someone had broken in and turned the place upside-down. Times were getting tough; he knew all the while thinking to himself as he set Joseph down on his bed that finding his wife and daughter before the trail cooled down was going to be a challenge. Rustler finally settled down next to Joseph's bed for a nap.

"It hurts so bad," Joseph cried.
Winston peeled off Josephs trousers and gently studied the bullet wound. It appeared the bullet passed through the truck door, enters Joseph's leg at the calf and then exited through, tearing a large portion of the leg muscle. It could have been worse Winston knew. The bullet could have split the calf muscle away from the tendon, but as it was now, Joseph would have to remain in bed until the healing process has a chance to take hold.
After rummaging through the pantry, Winston found what he needed to put together a compress bandage for his son's wound. Mary had made up some antibacterial salve earlier in the year when he had sliced open his hand accidentally while sharpening a knife. Iodine mixed with boiled sugarcane extract helped to protect from infection, and it was essential to survival in Winston's world where doctors were nowhere to be found. Infections from wounds added to the loss of many folks in Hartley. What seemed to be a small injury could easily fester into blood infections that would kill. Winston knew his son would need constant attention and that in a few days he would need to switch to using raw honey to aid in healing Joseph's wound.
Winston returned to Joseph's bedside with the bandages he prepared. Joseph was sweating and breathing hard. To see his son in so much pain dug deep into his heart, yet he didn't let it show.
The swelling in Joseph's leg was worsening, and now it had become nearly twice the size of his healthy left leg. Winston wrapped Joseph's leg with the medicated bandages he'd prepared earlier, while in the thought that the swelling was not a source of inflammation, but rather, swelling from the blunt force of an already mushroomed bullet passing through his calf.
"Now rest up son," Winston said, looking into Joseph's bloodshot eyes.
Joseph blinked his eyes a few times and mustered a weak smile, "Dad?"

"Yes?"

"What kind of bullet hit me?"

Winston knelt beside the bed and stared at his son a moment. Here was a little boy who was fast becoming a man. It had always been a mystery to Winston when the moment or time childhood fades from a person, and it dawned on him then, it was all about the circumstances of one's understanding. That one little moment when a child perceives the world the way it is; through the eyes of an adult and not that of a child.

Winston blinked a few times, and then said, "It was a pistol round."

"Did the slug pass through my leg?"

"Yes, Joseph. The bullet went through the door and through your calf."

Joseph mustered a smile. "The pain ain't so bad now Dad."

Winston swept his hand over his son's forehead. Joseph's temperature seemed fine. "That's a good sign, so try not to move your leg too much as it needs to heal."

He closed his eyes and gave a couple of quick nods. "I'm tired now."

"Yes, get some sleep," replied Winston with a chuckle, "I believe Rustler beat you to it. So while you two guys nap, I'll be close by straightening up the place."

* * *

It took Winston two hours to get everything back in order. Whoever came in while he and Joseph were gone came and left on foot. Only a few items from the pantry were gone, but everything else seemed in its place, albeit tossed onto the floor but still here nonetheless. Winston believed if the intruders had a vehicle, a lot more things would have been taken. As near as Winston could readily tell, only a jar of jelly and canned meat were missing. Winston kept a pillowcase filled with pemmican he had prepared a few years ago, and it too was missing. He was relieved in the thought that he still had a good portion packed away in his pickup truck along with some hardtack.

He was relieved to see the ancient arrow passed down to him from his forefathers was still mounted above the front door. It was the sign of a blessing of peace among the 5 Florida Indian Nations that went back over 500 years ago. It was the last remaining arrow of the Ponctoan Indian Tribe that vanished many centuries ago. The extinction of a people made such an impact on the Ais and Calusa Indian Nation that a truce was formed that never again they would war with one another. Someday, Winston would pass the ancient arrow to his son so that he may bless his new home and way of life.

Winston took down the arrow just to admire it once again. It was beautifully marked with yellow, purple and red stripes near the three feathers and with it a thin leather thong, characterizing it as a ceremonial piece. As if the saying 'if only this could talk,' applied to this arrow then it would tell him nothing more than what he already knew of it. It was made from the strength of wise birch tree and had the fletching of an eagle's feathers. The nock and the broad tip lay in the harmony of war, for if the arrowhead were aligning the bowstring, it would have been a hunting arrow. That he knew. He knew animal ribs ran vertical and all the more accessible for the arrow to pass between such ribs, but for a man, it was rib bones that ran horizontal and thus so with the arrowhead on this arrow.

AFTERMATH

The fire in the stove had lowered itself to the wood coals that glowed red now. A pot full of what would soon simmer into venison stew was placed on the stove, and now it was time to check on Joseph.

The disappearance of his wife and daughter were just one of the misfortunes that worried Winston but keeping busy helped with planning his next step. While it appeared Joseph was resting well, soon it would be time to fix a portion of that smoked pork that was wrapped and waiting in the truck just for Rustler. There was plenty of it, and Winston chopped a large piece into a bowl. Winston stopped a moment to smile at a memory of Darby getting a bath in this bowl when she was just a baby.

There was a large shank bone for Rustler and Winston decided to hide it on the front porch for later. After dropping the bone he gave it a nudge with his boot seeing it slide under the old weather-beaten wooden rocker, Winston sat down and then leaned forward to cup his face in his hands.

*** * * ***

The croaking of frogs didn't frighten Darby; even though it was now dark. Up ahead was the town's last building. It was the old gas station, dark and abandoned like everything else in town. She remembered poppa stopping there for gas many times in the past, and she loved to go inside because the gas station had a water fountain. It was the best water, icy cold like ice cream. Joseph would always make her wait her turn because he was older and bossy. Mister Fletcher owned the gas station and had an old fruit box just for her to stand on so she could reach the fountain water.

Darby stood in the darkened doorway that led inside the gas station office. There was the water fountain, and there was the fruit box just like she remembered. She swung her bag of goodies onto the desk where Mister Fletcher sat most of the time and dragged the fruit box over to the drinking fountain. Filled with excitement, she climbed up and pushed the button on the fountainhead, but no water came out. "Nothing works in this town!" she exclaimed.

"No matter," Darby huffed, jumping down from the fruit box and walking over to the big reclining chair behind the desk, "I'll just sit and wait for a customer!"

It was a large office chair, and after five or so minutes of rocking and singing, Darby curled-up in the chair and went to sleep.

CHAPTER 14

~Mrs. Edna Weatherly~

She lived all alone now, except for Billy who talked a lot but never spoke well enough for people to understand him; except for Edna Weatherly who understood everything he would say to her.

With the morning ritual, Edna would make breakfast for Billy and then head out with her basket to collect some eggs and wild blueberries that grew down on County Line Road. This was a good time of the year for berries, both blackberries, and blueberries. It was also good to see the sun peek out a little earlier too these days. It was safe to allow Billy to go out during the daytime because he wouldn't venture too far down the street, and of course, sneak around with that Jezebel down the road. Billy was not the responsible type and would get her pregnant and never own up to it.

Edna breathed a big sigh. It was about this same time last year or was it two when the angels came for Marsha. Edna's husband Sterling saw to it Marsha would be comfortable and saved Edna the pain of having to wish her a final goodbye. Perhaps it was this that broke Sterling's heart when he too passed on not long after that. Now it's just her and Billy left. Sometimes Edna thought that Billy never got over seeing her niece and husband pass away so suddenly. Edna thought it silly to think that someday they would come walking down County Line Road, hand in hand singing and laughing all the way home. Even if it were possible, she wouldn't mention a word of this to Billy. To get Billy's hopes high on the thought of seeing Marsha and Sterling come home would just be too cruel.

Edna was more than halfway up County Line Road with no berries to show for it. "Oh and no wonder," she laughed. "I pick a bushel of berries yesterday morning; shame on me."

She began to realize that this was all the farther down County Line Road she had gone. "Oh that's right," she said slapping herself on the forehead. "From here to Main Street, had to have lots more I didn't pick!"

AFTERMATH

There were a lot of blackberries to be picked which gave her the notion that the secret meadow with all the strawberries should be ready to pick by now. "Maybe tomorrow," she sighed. "My knees are not in the mood to pick strawberries today.

Besides, I have enough blackberries to make six-quart jars of jelly." Edna paused a moment, not sure she heard a little girls voice crying somewhere close by. The little voice came from off the shoulder of the main road leading into town, but where exactly was hard to tell; until Edna saw some tall grass move.

Edna crept along the shoulder of the road, her eyes ping-ponging warily as she moved through the tall grass. She stopped suddenly as she nearly stumbled over the small child sitting in the grass holding her little rubber sandal in one hand and fidgeting with the strap that apparently came loose from the sole.

"Marsha?"

Darby glanced over her shoulder, then back down to her sandal. "No, it's a flip-flop," she said with a sniff. "It's broken and keeps falling off my foot."

"Oh dear dear Marsha," Edna Weatherly said. "Come with me, and I'll make you your favorite pudding!"

Edna reached down and took the broken sandal. While Darby watched on, Edna pushed the sandal top thong back into place, then knelt and slipped the sandal on Darby's foot.

Darby's eyes grew wide, "You're not a stranger are you?"

Edna smiled, removed her babushka and shook free her silver-white hair. "Of course not darling; I'm your Auntie Edna."

Tilting her head, she looked up to Auntie Edna, "What ya got in the basket, Auntie Edna?"

"Blackberries," Auntie Edna replied. "Go ahead honey, have some. We'll eat them on the way home!"

Darby smiled and reached out her hand to Edna, and together they walked down County Line Road singing a song Darby's mother would sing to her while hanging up clothes from a basket on the clothesline.

A-tisket A-tasket, A green, and yellow basket.

I wrote a letter to my love, And on the way, I dropped it.

I dropped it, I dropped it. And on the way I dropped it, I dropped it I dropped it.

A little boy picked it up and put it in his pocket.

The blackberries were sweet and tasty this morning, and Darby ended up with a purple smile. Aunt Edna talked about all the fun things she had planned for them.

She had some crayons packed away with some old coloring books and dolls too. Doll clothes and even a dollhouse Uncle Sterling made a few years ago. She told Darby her and Billy were the only ones around nowadays and that much of the family didn't visit anymore because they lived so far away.

    Darby sat at the table eating biscuits and jelly. She brought up the things that bothered her now, and that was seeing her momma being taken away by bad men. "And Brother Jonas got shot in the face. I think he's okay now."
    Auntie Edna gasped while clutching her hand close about her own neck, "Why that is thee limit!" She rushed around to Darby's side of the table and knelt beside her chair, "Honey where do come up with such stories?"
    Darby just shrugged her shoulders and looked down at her plate of biscuit crumbs. Auntie Edna's attention drew to the plate of crumbs for a moment then sighed, "Honey would you like Auntie Edna to make you some pancakes?"
    "Huh?"
    She saw Darby had slipped away in deep thoughts about something that appeared to trouble her. "Now now," Edna spoke gently stroking Darby's hand. "We won't talk of such things; besides you'll scare Billy."
    Darby looked up and stole a glance at Billy who just stared back at her. He had a crazy look in his eyes which made Darby giggle. "Okay Billy, I won't scare you." She looked back to Auntie Edna, "Does he always stare like that?"
    "Oh, I wouldn't worry about him. He always stares and most of the time at no one. He just likes to stare a lot I suppose. And can you imagine, he told me he wanted to go to college the other day!"
    "You mean school?"
    "Yes," Auntie Edna replied, lowering her voice to a near whisper as if not wanting Billy to hear her. "I put him off telling him that I hadn't saved up the money enough for him to go to college, when the real truth is, he doesn't talk clear enough to be understood. Of course, I understand everything he says because he's my little boy."
    "Okay, Auntie Edna lets color!"
    "I'll get the crayons and coloring books!"

* * *

Throughout the evening and early morning hours, long before the sun came up that day, Mary Sawyer felt forced to hide away in the thick brush. Working slowly into the darkness of the woods off Tamiami Trail, she took cover from the sounds of

AFTERMATH

someone stalking her. The crack of twigs and the rustle of grass and dead leaves were all she knew of the stalker and a shadow she thought she saw earlier. Her instincts told her to burrow deeper into the woods, hoping at least the stranger would give up and turn back for the road.

Mary moved slowly, testing each footstep as she went, careful not to make a sound. Feeling something cold on her feet she realized she was walking into a small ditch full of water. Slowly moving on she tested the depth of the water with each step she took until finally, she came to the bank on the other side. There was a clearing beyond a small bulrush of trees, and she wasn't sure it was an area she could trust until daybreak when she could see a shopping plaza appear through the early morning fog. Apparently, she had crossed through a section of woods from Tamiami Trail to an intersection she now remembered seeing on the drive up to where she escaped the two idiots with the Oldsmobile.

The parking lot of the shopping plaza was enormous with the better half of the lot filled with abandoned cars.

Maybe, I can seek cover if needed in the thicket of all those cars. And perhaps that sporting goods store has shotgun shells lying around.

Mary suspected the stores had long been looted of useful items, just like in downtown Hartley. But she figured that in the event she found a few shotgun shells, it wouldn't be so far out of her way to go back for the shotgun she left behind leaning against the Oldsmobile. After the events of last night, she knew traveling without some form of protection was paramount to survival. She had heard there were desperate men all over the countryside looking to take advantage of anything they could. Mary pledged to herself that after all, she'd been through; she would never let anyone stand in her way of getting back home to her family.

While crossing the parking lot, her thoughts fell upon the pleasant memories she had of visiting a large shopping center like the one. Her and Winston would shop for a few items that weren't readily available in Hartley, like things for the truck and bow and arrow supplies and bowstring wax for Winston's crossbow, rifle, and gun ammunition and fishing supplies were just a few of the items. However best of all, was Linda's Fabrics store where Mary could pick up sewing supplies and bolts of fabric to make clothes and curtains and such. Thoughts as these brought a smile to Mary's face when she recalled the time they would all go for ice cream. Joseph would make fun of Darby because of all the ice cream on her face while at the same time Winston would laugh at Joseph and telling him he shouldn't be the one pointing his finger when he too had traces of chocolate syrup on his chin.

Mary paused just inside the door of the sporting goods store to allow her eyes to adjust to the darkened interior of the place. There was little in the way of a clear path to walk through the store as emptied displays and shelving littered the floor everywhere. Her head bobbed about looking for the area of the store where guns and ammunition were. As she recalled having been here before the economy collapsed, she, Winston and the kids remarked about the large Sail Fish mounted on the wall just to the right of the shelves where the gun case was. The fish was still there. And there was the case, smashed and emptied out of everything. Behind the case or counter was as she recalled stacks of rifles lined along the wall and they too were all gone.

Mary searched the drawers and all the litter strewn about looking for loose shotgun shells. She saw bullets here and there on the floor, but nothing that resembled shotgun shells. She found an arrow on the floor and picked it up. Using the arrow, she poked and prodded the piles of junk until she came upon a deflated rubber kayak and an assortment of hats and tee-shirts. She stopped and began to ponder over the trip home and how long that would take. Taking a hard look at the tee-shirts lying on the floor, she decided to take a few of them with her as the walk home may take as long as another two nights. She found a few shirts that had long-sleeves; those were her choice knowing how cold it got at night with the humidity so high as it was lately.

Under counters and under heavy display furniture Mary swept her arrow hoping to snag whatever items that may have gotten away from the previous looters who ransacked the store. Like a divining rod sensitive to water, the arrow swept out exactly what she hoped for; shotgun shells.

Five of them.

Mary dropped all five in her apron pocket. As she rose up from her hands and knees, her eyes caught a glorious site; the undisturbed rack of sports clothing. There were shirts, pants, jackets and hats of all sizes and colors, but mostly items that had a camouflage print. She found a pair of camouflage trousers that fit, matching shirts and a hunter's vest with many pockets and zippers. It now dawned on her the many opportunities to clothe her children crossed her mind. If it was all still here when she returned with Winston, they could surely make use of these clothing items. And the prospect of safely getting home became bright when Mary discovered a pair of new hunting boots.

CHAPTER 15

~*The Sawyer Homestead*~

The swelling in Joseph's right calf had not gone down, but in fact became noticeably worse. Winston remained cheerful around his son; however, he feared infection was beginning to set in and now finding a way to draw out the toxic fluids in the wound he would have to prepare the herbal medicine needed in making a plaster bandage.

It was darker than usual as the overhead skies had begun filling with the threat of storm clouds. Winston lit a few lamps as he went about the task of mixing and boiling up a batch of much-needed medicine. In a barrel just off the kitchen porch entry was rendered fat. He scooped a cup of the lard into cast iron skillet and cracked a chunk of salt he kept in a bin next to the barrel of lard and added it to the skillet before reentering the kitchen. In another skillet he set a mixture of goldenseal and aloe pulverized together to make a slurry. Mixing everything together, Winston stripped some old but clean rags made from discarded clothing in a basket kept by the root cellar bin. Plopping a long strip of cotton tee-shirt material in a pot he had sitting in the sink, Winston worked the pitcher pump arm a few times bringing about a water level to cover the cotton material completely.

By the time the pot began boiling; Winston had finished frying up some eggs, grits, and sliced cornbread for breakfast. Rustler followed by his nose, wandered into the kitchen in time to see his bowl hit the floor with his meal of pork and chopped bean snaps.

Joseph was sitting up in bed when Winston came through the door of the bedroom. A little small-talk about how Joseph was feeling and a promise to return with bandages to change-out after breakfast; at which point Winston felt Joseph was running a slight fever, and that revelation indicated infection was setting in.

Winston was back in the kitchen getting the bandage plaster together. Rustler had already banged his way out the front door, leaving the door-spring to slam closed behind him as he headed out to explore the woods. Making his way back to the bedroom, Winston took a small flask of alcohol along with a large towel from the kitchen. After taking a seat on the bed, Winston explained that he was going to change Joseph's bandage and that he was going to flush the wound with medicine that will sting like a thousand bee stings.

Winston handed Joseph a small toy. It was an action figure made out of rubber, "Bite down on this," he told his son. Winston raised Joseph's injured leg and tucked a towel under it to collect the runoff. "Ok, ready, here we go!"

Holding his son's leg down at the ankle with one hand, Winston slowly poured the alcohol with the other. Joseph's jaws clamped down on the action figure while letting out a sharp rising moan which turned to a blood-curdling scream and while Joseph gasped trying to collect himself from the pain, Winston poured the rest of the alcohol on the other side of the leg where the exit wound was. The boy was ripping at the sheets with his hands when his father dabbed the wounds dry with a second clean towel.

Winston had finished up wrapping the plaster bandages on Joseph's leg while the boy's sides heaved from the pain which was now beginning to subside. However, having fed Joseph before dressing his wounded leg had been a mistake as Winston watched his son lean off to the side of his bed and wretched on the floor. Winston left and returned with a glass of water, and then went for a scrub pail and mop.

When Winston returned, Joseph apologized for throwing up on the floor but told him he wouldn't have to clean it up as he pointed to Rustler who had entered the house through Joseph's open window. They both grimaced as Rustler happily took over the cleaning operation, and then laughed together while Rustler sat looking at them with an expression of wonder. He then lifted his hind paw to scratch behind his ear.

Joseph discussed his worries about his missing mother and sister, and Winston tried to ease his concerns by telling him, he was in control and would eventually track them down. Joseph looked up to his father knowing he had all the faith in the world for his father's abilities to be successful. The only thing that worried Winston now was that the trail was getting colder by the minute and that having his son who needed his undivided care and attention, the likelihood of getting back on the hunt for his family would have to start again today. What he could only hope for his son was that he could be relied upon to stay behind safe and secure while letting his leg get the chance to heal. Seeing how his son was beginning to show cognizance, he felt the time right to get back on the hunt for his family.

Rustler rose up and began to itch behind his ear for the fifth time in five minutes. Winston glanced over to Rustler, "What did you get into Rustler?"

Joseph spoke, "It looks like he might have lots of fleas or something."

Winston stood up from the spot on the bed where he'd been sitting, and as he did, he noticed a freshly killed rabbit lying on the floor by the window where Rustler jumped through to get inside of Joseph's bedroom.

"Well, I see Rustler brought home some lunch!"

Holding up the rabbit for Joseph to see, Winston continued, "And also a bunch of fleas."

AFTERMATH

    Lifting the rabbit up Winston saw the animal's fur was loaded with fleas. He quickly tossed the rabbit through the window. "Looks like I have a few chores to do before I can leave," said Winston shaking his head. "First let's get that rabbit cleaned and ready for the pot, and then I know someone in this room needs a flea bath!"
    Prior to cleaning Rustler and the rabbit he brought home, Winston went to his bedroom and dug through a box of books, choosing 'Life on the Mississippi River,' for his son to read. It was one of Winston's favorite books growing up, and he knew his son would enjoy it.

    Winston was surprised to see Rustler enjoying his flea bath. Maybe it was getting the personal attention or just the water, or both that excited Rustler. He took off running for the pond down the road just as soon as Winston finished with him. An hour later, and after Winston had dressed-out the rabbit for the pot, he set the outdoor fire pit ablaze and carefully lowered the stew pot on the grating to cook. There were carrots, corn, and potatoes to add and he took the time to have those vegetables prepared and ready to drop into the stew pot on his way out to search for his wife and daughter. He knew that both Joseph and Rustler would want to tag along with him, but he thought it best to have Joseph remain in bed keeping his leg at rest to allow the healing process to continue. Also, Winston felt having Rustler stay with Joseph, was the wisest decision to make after sensing that the homestead had been trespassed a few days ago. There were noises last night, not commonly heard outside around the property, and Winston was sure the prowlers were watching his place. He heard Rustler leave during the night and knew the dog had kept the peace with merely his presence about.
    Winston had all but finished the last chore before setting out on the trail; stoking the fire pit with a couple of split oak logs and tossing the vegetable into the pot to simmer, he walked back to the house to let Joseph know he'd be home by sunset. However, making his way back to the house, he was greeted by Rustler. Again, Rustler was proud to show Winston the selection of his newly caught dinner fare. It was a snapping turtle the size of a car's hubcap! Rustler had the turtle clenched between his jaws, and as it was discovered by Winston, the snapping turtle had Rustlers right ear grasped between his jaws as well. Rustler seemed to know not to drop the turtle on the ground, mainly because the turtle would lead him around by the ear, and Rustler didn't like being leashed and led around.
    "Good boy," Winston told Rustler as he patted the dog on the head. And even though he knew Rustler was in pain, he managed to shake his tail. Winston withdrew his hunting knife from the sheath attached to his belt and zipped the turtle's head away from its neck. "Sorry boy, the head will have to stay latched on your ear for a little while."

Winston knew the turtle's head was still alive and wouldn't let go of Rustler's ear until the sun went down. Why that was, was beyond Winston's grasp of a reasonable explanation, but in his experiences, with wild game, this was more of a rule than an exception. Perhaps it had something to do with the head drying out and the jaw tendons shrinking that allowed for the turtle's head to release its grip.

He stood petting Rustler while he recalled the time a few years back when a snapping turtle latched onto his hand while noodling for catfish. He didn't know which hurt worse, the jaws of the turtle cutting through the tissues of his hand or the pressure of the animal's jaws.

Winston didn't feel he had the time to clean and dress a turtle and did what came naturally to him, and that was to slide the whole turtle onto an open portion of the fire pit grate to slow cook inside its shell with the idea he'd feed it to Rustler later. Rustler danced around circling around his feet. He seemed to know that Winston was about to fetch him a doggy chew treat that he had nailed to the side of his shed to dry. He waited patiently while he drew out the nail and checked on one of the hog ears he had dehydrating on the shed. The ear was dry and stiff; too stiff to bend. It was tough and ready to chew. It was perfect.

Rain began to fall as Winston and Rustler ducked onto the porch. Dark clouds filled the sky, and it appeared that the storm would be with them most if not all day. Inside the house was dark as night and Winston lit a few table lamps, thinking all the while that it would also lend an appearance of someone being home while he was away. Rustler had already found his favorite spot next to Joseph's bed. He was content to sit there chewing on his pig's ear chew toy when Joseph looked up to his dad, "What's that on Rustler's ear?"

"A turtle head," Winston replied. "He's fine with it for now, but I have to tell you that he'll be here while I'm away for the remainder of the day. I brought you a pitcher of sweet orange flavored water and a strip of momma's taffy on the bed stand."

Joseph smiled, and he could hear him tell Rustler that he'd read him a story about 'Life on the Mississippi.'

Winston pulled out to the access road behind his homestead and stopped to check his 9mm Ruger semi-automatic pistol for a full magazine and then cocked an loaded his pistol crossbow with a bolt (arrow,) read to fly. For a small crossbow, this 80 lb. weapon packed a powerful and deadly punch at close range. It was his favorite for fishing Tilapia which were abundant in ponds and Nile perch that gathered about bass fish hatching beds at night. Winston had learned his lesson when his son was shot that he would be armed and ready for an ambush at any time.

AFTERMATH

Chapter 16

~Mary Sawyer~

Mary was making her way through the parking lot outside the strip mall. With her, she carried a bag of items, mostly clothing and a few other items of interest, including a disposable lighter and a small assortment of razor-sharp broad-tip arrow points like the one on the arrow she had found in the store. She figured these razor sharp tips could be useful in cutting small twigs for tonight's campfire. These arrow tips were clumsy and dangerous to use for cutting things, so she brought along the arrow to use as a tool to safely handle using them like a knife.

 She was not afraid of going deep within the forest and building the sort of campsite like her husband had done in the past. She enjoyed those days of camping in the woods with the children and looked upon the experience as nothing to be afraid of. The only difference was she had no way of preparing a meal for herself, however, with the soda can she found, she knew she could at least boil some water to drink. She still had her can opener, and that was something she was glad to have taken with her.

 Moving along the rows of derelict cars and trucks Mary froze in her tracks when she heard a noise as if a hubcap popped loose and strike the pavement. Then the sound of someone grunting followed by a muffled voice cursing over what Mary now determined was a man removing a tire from a car opposite of where she was standing. He was on the other side of the car, and Mary peeked around the front of the car to get a look at person removing the tire. It was a foolish move on her part when she realized she had cast a shadow on the stranger.

 He was on his knees removing the lug nuts when suddenly distracted by her shadow that he snapped his head back and looked up to her in surprise. Mary immediately recognized the man. He was the stranger who walked up on her yesterday evening, and now it appeared he was taking a tire to replace the flat tire on the Oldsmobile. There was a specific potential good to what he was doing yet; on the other hand, it could spell trouble in the end. If he was a good man and was willing to give her a ride home once he changed the tire, which indeed would serve her well, then she was ready to open a dialogue with him.

 Mary smiled at him knowing that if he meant her harm, she could easily outrun a man rolling a spare tire through the woods.

 "I guess you figured out what I am doing here right?"

 Mary sighed, taking a moment to study his expression, "You're fixing to replace the tire on my car so that you can steal it."

 "Can't lie, ma'am," he said pointing to the Oldsmobile emblem on the car. "The bolt pattern matches your car because it is an Oldsmobile. As far as stealing it, I'd have to say that there are salvage laws in place. I figured you abandoned your car which puts it up for grabs on the salvage market. First come first serve you know."

 "No, you just figure because the car runs that it was worth your while to steal it. Am I wrong?"

"So what's the car worth to you?"

"I'll make it an even trade for that pistol you took last night."

The stranger frowned and then looked back down to his work. "I don't think so."

"Ok, then. I'll make you a deal since it is my car – and,"

"It ain't your car," the stranger interrupted. "I have the keys, and that makes me the owner. After all, possession is 9/10 of the law."

Mary was getting frustrated and angry with this skinny 'scare-crow' of a man. He had a hooked shaped nose and beady eyes, and he could smile in several different ways, and she was not happy with the smile he was showing her right now. She thought better of calling him a *shit-stick*, but then again she figured she would play along with his little game of words. "Okay," Mary said. "According to you, I own 1/10 of that car, and I say I will sell my share of that vehicle for a ride home. Deal?"

The stranger acted as if he didn't hear her. He angrily shook the car back and forth trying to dislodge the tire. Mary could see that if this moron had used a jack to lift the vehicle, the tire would have been easier to remove without presenting a potential danger to him. "It would probably be a good idea if you would help me here," he said with a sigh of resignation. "I don't have enough ass on me to shake this tire free of the car if you know what I mean?"

Without saying a word, Mary put her weight into the job of wiggling the front of the car back and forth while asking if he decided her offer was a deal he would accept. The stranger slid down in front of the tire and with both legs straddling the wheel, he wiggled the tire trying to get the lug studs to slip through the tire rim. "I'll think about it," he huffed.

Mary gave the car a hard shove, and with that effort, the tire popped free. Without the support of the tire, the vehicle dropped abruptly pinning the stranger legs under the front axle. Hearing the stranger's agonizing scream, she dashed around to his side of the vehicle. Her heart pounded as she frantically tried to pull him free. She stooped behind him; her arms under his while she struggled to yank him out from under the car. She tugged and tugged and with each tug brought the most dreadful of all screams she had ever experienced.

"Oh Jesus," he cried, wringing his hands. "Aaah, oh lord, aaah!"

Mary grimaced. She became horror-struck to see the car's hub and axle mashing his legs flat. Blood was beginning to pool-out from under his crushed legs, and she knew he was going to bleed out. She was breathing heavy when she told him she was going to get him out. "But first I need to stop your bleeding." She lifted his shirt and released his belt on his pants, pulling it free. Her mind raced ahead while she applied his trouser belt as a tourniquet to the one leg she felt strongly was the one doing the heavy bleeding. "I'm going to get a jack to lift this car," she told him, hoping this car had its jack in the car.

"Ok," he said with a weak smile and a wink of his eye. "I'll wait here."

The pain seemed to have gone away, she thought. *He's already in shock!*

Inside the car, there were no keys to be found. Using her can opener, she managed to pry-out the trunk lock, but still, the trunk remained latched close. It was then she remembered back in the day when she and her brother snuck into the drive-in theater by stowing away in the trunk of her daddy's car. Her daddy would

AFTERMATH

just pop the back seat loose, and they got out of the trunk without having to raise the trunk lid and arouse anyone's suspicion.

Mary figured out how to release the rear seat back, and now after 30 minutes, she was dragging out a bumper jack. The stranger had done a lot for the condition he reluctantly found himself in. He had managed to introduce himself as Mel and had recited every prayer that was taught to him in Sunday school as a young boy growing up in his neck of the woods. In fact, he recounted them all several times. And times being what they were, he had a family he was trying to get home to see, so he decided to step things up a bit by coaching Mary how to set up the jack. Just as she was ready to begin work the jack into place, she noticed Mel had just urinated in his pants, and she pretended not to notice as she respected this man's dignity. He closed his eyes for what seemed a bit longer than she felt comfortable with while he drew a few breaths and then reopened his eyes. A feeble expression of worry creased his face as he looked up to her and said he was ready for her to lift the car.

Feeling that she had raised the car far enough off Mel, she went over to him and told him she was going to drag him over to sit in a shady place nearby. However, she was stunned to see his other leg begin bleeding far worse than the one she had strapped a tourniquet on. It seemed the weight of the car had pinched off the supply of blood in this particular leg, and now that she had lifted the car and moved him, the blood began to flow profoundly from an artery in his leg. Mary tried to use the belt she had on one leg and strap both legs together to squeeze off the flow of blood, but that idea failed to work. Mel cried he didn't want to die, but it was apparent that he would if Mary didn't act fast. She rummaged through the contents of her bag for the tee-shirt she had gotten from the sporting goods store. Using the shirt from one as a tourniquet and the belt on the other, she eased the flow of blood, the best she could. Now, she and Mel were streaked in blood from hands up to the elbows. Mary now sat alongside Mel, it was all she could do for him now, and that was to stay with him for a while.

"Mary, I'm sorry for giving you such a hard time about the car."

"I understand Mel," Mary said. "Times are hard, and everyone has to look out for themselves I guess."

"I've been blessed knowing you, even if it is for a short while."

Mary took his hand. "I truly wished this never happened."

"That makes the two of us."

"Mel?"

"Yes."

"If you let me have the keys to *our* car, I promise I come back and bring you home with me so that you can get care for your legs."

Mel just bobbed his head and lifted his hand to point to where his backpack was sitting. "No, go ahead Mary. The keys and your gun are in there. Take them and don't worry about me. I'll be fine."

Mary's eyebrows drew a straight line in disbelief, "No you won't! I'm coming back for you."

He sighed. "Well, if you insist, I'd rather you visit with my wife and children and tell them I loved them very much and had hoped to have made it home."

Mel dug his wallet out of his pocket and took out his driver's license. "My home address is here. Follow Tamiami Trail north to Connor road; it's about 20 miles up, and there's a 30-foot fiberglass figure of a lady in a yellow dress holding up a car tire on the corner of Conner road ... make a left and my house is two blocks down on the right."

"A 30-foot woman holding a car tire?"
"Yeah, believe it or not. It's a tire store."
Mary thought about that a moment before asking, "Mel you're asking me to ... hold that thought!"
With little time on her side, she jumped up and told Mel she'd be back real soon. She took the backpack leaving her shopping bag of goodies behind while she grabbed the spare tire and rolled it down to the path she'd used to get here; through the woods to the road and north to the Oldsmobile. She was surprised at her own progress. Half expecting to get hung up in the woods and having to tote the heavy tire most of the way, but she felt lucky, or was it adrenaline? Through the adversary of overcoming the negativity she held in her heart, she now rejoiced at the sight of the old car ahead. However, there was just one problem with this. Something didn't appear right.

Mary froze in her tracks.

She searched Mel's backpack for the 38 special revolver. She rolled the cylinder out and checked the weapon for bullets. All 5 rounds were present, and there were much more in the Oldsmobile if those two men who she watched ransacking the car didn't get to them yet. *There'll be no way they will take those bullets.*

Mary kept the pistol close to her side as she rolled up the last 50 yards to the Oldsmobile where she watched one of the two men inspecting the shotgun and scratching his head.

The two men snapped to attention the moment they saw Mary, "Leave," she told them. "Leave NOW."

As far as she could tell they were unarmed, however, that didn't mean anything to her as she was outnumbered and they knew they had that advantage twice over. "Oh we'll leave alright," the curly haired man said laughing. "When we get what we want."

"Oh, you don't leave, and you will get what you don't want. Now go away as I have work to do and I don't have time to play games."

Mary was short on words at this point, so when the one man began walking toward her, she pulled her pistol up and shot him. The other man ran around to the front of the car where his buddy fell shot in the shoulder and screaming and told Mary to drop the gun. He held the empty shotgun at her and told her to surrender the weapon.

Mary aimed her pistol at him and told him it would be the last time he breathed air if he didn't leave with his friend. "Leave your friend behind, and I'll finish him off with a round in the head, got it?"

The thought of not knowing where Darby was at this moment and whether the child was safely home, tore at her heart. Time was everything, and this *asshole* was stealing away her family, and she was becoming livid.

Perhaps the man could see the way she stood, arms streaked in blood, and the rage in her eyes and knew she was ready to kill him where he stood. He threw down the shotgun and helped his friend on his feet. Together they headed down the road. Sadly it came to her after now realizing she shot a man in the shoulder when she was aiming for his head that Winston needed to take the time with her and give her some target shooting advice.

Chapter 17

~Billy Weatherly~

Edna Weatherly was astonished at Billy's behavior and attitude around Darby. Usually, Billy was shy and withdrawn from new acquaintances and often would hide in Marsha's room. However now it seemed he was happy to see Marsha home again and the two played together nicely. Billy even played 'house' with Marsha, allowing himself to be the baby of the family. Never before would Billy allow himself to be pushed around in a baby carriage or even dressed up like a baby.

It was heartwarming for Edna to see Billy become part of the family again. In fact, his appetite seemed to improve. Now if she could just get him to eat all his vegetables. "I say," Edna smiled shaking a finger in Billy's face. "You eat so much chicken, I'm afraid you're gonna fly away some day."

"I love chicken," yelled Darby from the kitchen table.

"Don't we all honey, don't we all."

"Auntie Edna, when are you going to show me the henhouse? I never picked eggs before because momma doesn't want us kids to get lice!"

"Tsk tsk," Edna replied. "I will have to send you home with a spare shower cap. Auntie Edna has a whole drawer full of them!"

"You mean tomorrow, we can pick eggs?"

"Honey, the word to use is *gathering* eggs. You don't pick them you gather them in a basket." Edna's eyebrows rose suddenly as a thought came to her mind. "I will show you how to gather eggs and while you practice that, Auntie Edna is going to harvest some honey from the beehives."

"Harvest is like the word *gathering*, right Auntie Edna?"

"That's right Marsha!"

Darby gave a big smile and then asked, "Why do they call me Darby at home?"

Edna gave it a little thought. "Well you know, I don't know. I do think it's almost certainly a nickname. Your uncle Sterling had a nickname; did you know that?"

Darby's eyes grew wide, "He did? Tell me, Auntie Edna."

Edna laughed when she began to recall how her husband Sterling ended up with a name like Oscar. "Well, you see; when Uncle Sterling was just a little boy, his two older brothers thought that if he begged for money to go to the picture show, his parents would gladly give it to him because he was a cute little boy. So when he returned to tell the brothers, they wouldn't give him any money they sent him back two or three times to ask again and again. Finally, around the third time when they asked him to go back and ask for money, Sterling cried saying, 'I keep osking and osking and they keep saying no!' So that's how he got the nickname Oscar!"

Darby laughed and clapped her hands, "Oh I get it now."

Many hours later, after coloring and storybook time, Darby asked if she could stay over because she was scared of being left alone outside walking along a dark road. "Unless I can have Billy walk me home, right Billy?"
Edna turned a glowering expression toward Billy, "Don't make promises you can't keep Billy."
"But Auntie Edna," Darby pleaded, "Please?"
"Billy can't be trusted out in the night, and besides, he's yellow. If a machine comes down the road, he could cause you both to get hit."
Darby looked over to Billy with a confused look on her face. "But Auntie Edna, Billy isn't yellow."
"Oh honey, that's just an expression for being a coward! There are a lot of things about Billy you don't understand. He wasn't expected to live for one and for another; he may have suffered brain damage. I know how hard that is to understand now, but if you would have seen him as a baby, you'd understand." Edna beamed with pride, "I was the first one he saw when he finally opened his eyes."
Darby got up from the chair at the table and went over and hugged Edna. "But Billy is okay now Auntie Edna. Don't cry."
"He's all I have now," Edna sobbed.
"But you have me, and I'll come to visit every chance I get. Maybe we can bake Billy a happy birthday cake!"
Edna's sad face turned cheerful, "Oh my, I am so glad you reminded me. Billy's birthday is tomorrow. Isn't that right Billy?"
Billy tried to ignore the conversation, but Darby saw a little smile come over Billy when they talked about birthday cakes. "You know what they say about happy birthday cake Billy?" Billy turned a look toward Darby, "Happy birthday cakes are the best cakes ever!"
Edna whispered in Darby's ear so that Billy would overhear her tell Darby that they'll make Billy's favorite birthday gift together. "You know Billy first bed was a potholder, he was that tiny when he was born. And ever since then he takes my potholders when I'm not looking. I find them under where he is sleeping most of the time. So tomorrow while the cake is baking, we'll make one for him as a birthday gift."
"We will?"
"Yes, and I'll show you how to make them, won't that be fun?"
Darby beamed, "Oh yes Auntie Edna, oh yes. Tomorrow will be such a happy day."

Darby stared out the window. A storm was raging, and the wind was bending the tall grass. "Auntie Edna?"
"Yes, honey."
"Can I say over?"
"Of course you may."

* * *

Winston left his truck parked down the road from the house he, Joseph, and Rustler had been the day before. He concealed his presence in the woods across from the house, studying the grounds for any activity. The beat-up Oldsmobile was not

AFTERMATH

around, yet sooner or later it may appear, so Winston dug into his position behind a pile of concrete and bricks that had once made up the foundation of a home long gone. A small circular array of brick marked the location of an old well. A tiny wisp of smoke rose from the opening of the well. The odor of charred wood and garbage filled the air. Apparently, here was the place surviving members of the area dump and burned household trash.

As it had been most of the day, the storm had subsided to a light drizzle, and the wind would die down before another wave of heavy rain and wind would set in. Even so, it seemed all was quiet, and Winston reached beneath his rain poncho for his binoculars. Scanning the view to the house across the street revealed all was quiet; nothing moved except the rain.

Breaking the silence was Winston's truck as it drove by.

Winston made his way out of the woods to the road just in time to see his truck disappear behind an old farmhouse. Immediately he began scanning the homestead for signs of his truck. However, the distance was too great to ascertain proof his truck did not circle out to an off-road trail he knew of.

Immediately Winston began tracking down his truck, hoping he could follow any tracks left behind before the next band of heavy rain and wind concealed them. He went back, picked up his compound crossbow and then returned to the road; heading off down to the old farmhouse nearly a mile away.

What was once a paved road had become overgrown with grass and even small trees. Even so, Winston could make out the traces of his truck's tires. Perhaps his truck had been the only vehicle that had gone down this part of the road in ages. He recalled having gone down this road a few years ago, and the only thing down the road from here was a large sand pit and a few hunting trails. He had bagged a deer or two from this area long ago, and began to wonder if the men who had stolen his truck were living in on of a few hunters' shacks, he recalled seeing back then. Either way, Winston was pretty sure no trails were leading out.

Having lost his truck to thieves didn't concern him at this point. He knew sooner or later he would get his truck back. The only concern right now was staying on the trail until that time came. Winston needed to get back home to his son, and if he failed to reclaim his truck, he would have to turn and walk home. It would take the better part of an hour to walk home, and as Winston figured with the sun setting in a little over two hours, he had perhaps an hour to gamble on finding his truck. At that turning point in time, Winston feared to lose his truck forever.

When Winston came to the old abandoned farmhouse, his truck was nowhere to be seen. He moved his crossbow around his shoulder by the strap and lowered the weapon down in front of him. The rope cocking device he kept handy, slung around his neck was removed and hooked in place on the bowstring. He placed his boot into the nose stirrup of the crossbow and gave the rope cocking device and upward pull; latching the bowstring into the trigger mechanism with a distinct click. Any man who would make an effort to break in and hotwire another man's truck was a dangerous man to consider, he thought silently. Winston slid a 420 grain broad tipped arrow into his compound crossbow. He had recalled killing large dear and black bears, with most of those kills from distances up to 50 yards away with this very bow. It was powerful and highly accurate with its laser 3 dot reflective scope.

Feeling he was ready now, he followed the hunting trail into the woods. Telltale tracks from his truck showed it had pulled up some of the tall grass on its way into the forest. He quietly followed along, not making a sound as he kept all senses alerted for noise and movement. The old hunting cabin came into view, and so did his truck, so Winston moved off the trail to the thick of the woods surrounding the cabin. He could hear voices, and from what he heard from an exchange inside the cabin the conversation was between two men; one of which exited the cabin to urinate.

Winston popped the lens covers from his compound bow scope and rotated the knob on the scope, turning on the laser. He poked around the trunk of a large pine tree while assessing the distance to be about 40 yards to the target. Taking aim on the urinating man, Winston put the center dot on the area between the man's shoulder blades. A split second after firing his compound crossbow the heard the dull thud of the bolt (arrow) penetrating the urinating man's back.

Winston never took the time to study the situation but rather recocked his crossbow and set another bolt. He knew the bolt he'd just fired passed straight through the urinating man because a second sound of the bolt burrowing into a tree not far in front of the target shown a glimpse of blue and white arrow fletching sticking out of that tree.

Winston waited.

The urinating man had fallen dead without making a sound, and for the next several minutes all was quiet. From inside the cabin, a voice called out, "Lester, you going to hang around out there in the rain and take a bath?"

It was a low raspy voice of a man, and Winston knew he'd be coming out the door to find his friend dead. What he didn't expect was the man was holding the shotgun he had left in his truck. Winston saw the barrel of the shotgun first as the man gingerly pushed through the doorway of the cabin to have a look around, "Lester?"

Winston leveled the compound crossbow and placed the center laser dot on the man's head and fired. The man sagged under the strain of the bolt that pinned his head to the heavy wooden timber of the door frame. Winston reached down and withdrew his 9 mm semi-automatic pistol from his holster under his rain poncho and slowly approached the man in the doorway. He was close enough to see through the door while retrieving his shotgun, that there was no one else inside.

Winston stood silent for a moment. There was not enough remorse in him to give these two thieves a decent burial. They got what they deserved, he knew. They knew the consequences of robbing folks of life-sustaining goods. His life and every member of his family's life depended on this truck, and he felt justified in protecting his family with whatever it took.

He tossed his compound crossbow and shotgun on the front seat of his pickup truck. The three wires that were cut; he twisted back together, then used his key and started the truck.

* * *

AFTERMATH

The rain had gone to a drizzle, and the road up ahead seemed different in a way that made Winston's heart pound. Heavy smoke filled the air, and when he drove closer, he discovered the smoke was coming from his home. Or rather, the charred remnants that were once his home.

Frightened of what he might find, he stopped and got out of his truck, but his knees became weak, and he felt it difficult to pull himself together and discover what he feared the most. While leaning on the hood of his truck, Winston closed his eyes, his mind in the anguish that he may have been the one who started this fire leaving the stove unattended; and the firebox left open to spit an ember onto the floor.

Tormented in the idea that he never left the firebox open but he couldn't be absolutely sure that he didn't. Having made his way to the porch, he came upon the lifeless body of a man; his throat torn out, he lied staring blankly up at the sky. It became clear to him that this man had not made his way out of the house before Rustler took him down. As he entered the house, he noticed a kerosene table lamp lying on the floor, blackened and still warm to the touch. It was one of two lamps he left lit in the house when he left and apparently what caused the fire. The scene that played-out in Winston's mind was that this man entered the house not expecting to be met by Rustler. A struggle ensued, and the table lamp was knocked to the floor resulting in the fire.

CHAPTER 18

~Mary Sawyer changes a tire~

Now that the rain eased up, Mary was eager to get on the road and away from the two bloated corpses nearby. The old Oldsmobile was in poor shape but proved to be reliable. After making a few quick changes like ripping out the old and sagging headliner and adjusting the seat, Mary was on her way back to the parking lot to pick up Mel.

It felt good to be moving along at a faster clip than walking and feeling the fresh air on her face. She thought about what it would be like to just put Mel out of her mind and head straight home, but she knew she would never be able to rest at night knowing she had left a guy to suffer and die slowly. True, she recalled him saying to her to leave him with a request she would seek out his family and deliver the news that he loved them and wouldn't be coming home. This affected her in a way that she felt she needed to fulfill his request. After all, she hoped that if she or Winston were in a dire situation, someone would step up and grant the last wish. Thinking about this brought a whole new meaning to how important his final request was. Dead or alive, Mary was determined to deliver Mel home to his family.

When Mary arrived back at the place she had left Mel, she discovered he was still alive, but barely able to hold his head up. He had lost too much blood, and this she knew: Mel may not make the 20 or 30-mile trip home. Even so, Mary did the best she could, dragging Mel up and into the car despite having to rest a few minutes in between getting him over and then pulling him into the car's passenger side seat from her position on the driver's side. With tears in her eyes, she went around to the passenger's side door and carefully lifted his mangled legs into the car and closed the door.

A 30-foot woman was standing on the corner street, just as Mel had described earlier. The colossal woman statue of fiberglass held high a gigantic car tire. This, as Mary recalled from Mel's instructions earlier that morning was Conner Road. Making a left onto Conner, Mary counted two houses down on the right and pulled into the driveway. A miniature Border collie raced up to the car wagging its tail.

AFTERMATH

Before she could get out of the car, a woman wearing an apron with printed daisies on it stepped out onto the porch. Two children roughly the age of Joseph and Darby followed. Mary could see Mel's likeness in the little girl and knew she came to the right house.

"It's your husband Mel," Mary began as she closed the distance between her and Mel's wife June. "He's hurt real bad and lost a lot of blood."

Mary saw June's mouth sag open and her eyebrows furrow as she bobbed her head around to get a glimpse of the old Oldsmobile behind Mary. "Let me call Mel Junior up from the garden out back," June said.

Trailing back to the car, Mary checked Mel to see if he were still alive. He seemed deadly still, his chin resting down on his chest, hand resting in his lap. In a near whisper, Mary told Mel he was home. To her surprise, Mel raised a sigh, and his head lifted a bit but then dropped to rest again on his chest; evident to Mary that he was too weak to respond.

Mel's two children had followed up behind Mary, both eager to see their father. Mary told them as they both peered through the window that their father was hurt bad and that he needed to hear them talk.

"Daddy," said the little girl, "are you going to get better?"

"Yeah, Pop, you said we'd go fishing when you got back," said the little boy.

It was a great effort on Mel's part to raise his head, and while he did put forth the energy to do so, he rested his head to one side nearest the window and opened his eyes. He didn't say anything; he just smiled contently saying that he was home now and that is where he'd stay. His three or four-day scavenger hunts were over, and although he didn't say it, his days of fishing over too.

Mel passed away just then, and even so, the children kept talking to him.

"Does it hurt daddy?"

"I think Pop's dead," the little boy said, his eyes filling with tears.

June arrived, never getting the chance to see Mel while he was alive. She stood by the children while they clung to her crying. June's eyebrows arched and her hand held over her mouth, quietly sobbed. Mel Junior stood in silent disbelief, his hands at his side. "Mom," Junior said, "I know how hard this is, but we need to get the kids in the house while we talk amongst ourselves.

In the moments that followed June returned to talk with her eldest son who looked to Mary as a healthy young man in his late teens. "Mom, we're going to move dad to the table in the dining room where we can prepare him for burial."

Mary helped get Mel in the house and then offered to be of help in any way possible. Junior left the house promptly and sat on the steps of the porch outside.

She knew he wanted to be alone at this time and when June told Mary to go home to her family, she hugged June and told her she had a beautiful family and that Mel was proud of them all.

"He felt the need to wander a few days at a time," she told Mary. "He'd come home with wonderful things he found and would hang out with the kids a week or two and then be off again."

Mary left the house and found Junior had left, so before going, she wanted to see that he was going to be alright. She saw him out back in the barn hoisting down some lumber from a loft above a work area filled with old farm implements and tools. He stopped to talk with Mary about his father. She had seen he was crying, his eyes red and a sniff or two gave it away when he said he was fine.

He pointed to an old rusty tractor just outside the barn. "That tractor was Dad's pride and joy, even though it doesn't work; but he worked on it all the time." Junior chuckled and sniffed. "He used to say that old tractor was going to kill him in the end, and when it did, he wanted to be buried under it."

With a half-smile, Mary stared at the old tractor, "So I take it we're laying dad to rest under a tractor?"

Junior nodding his head, "Yep, and just as soon as I build him a decent coffin and dig the hole, we'll pay our last respects to a great man. I'll push the old tractor over his grave just like he wanted it."

"I'll help."

"No ma'am," Junior quickly replied. "I've got to do this myself."

Junior had it all figured out, right down to the rope handles on the coffin, and later as the sun was on the horizon, Mary headed home.

* * *

Joseph's bedroom, though in better shape than the rest of the house was empty. No Joseph. No Rustler. Winston breathed with the uneasy thought that included kidnapping. However, that too made no sense. If there had been two intruders, then what about the one dead at the door? Perhaps Rustler was busy with that one while the other grabbed Joseph and made a getaway. Rustler's disappearance, in this case, was due to him chasing down the kidnapper?

Winston rubbed his forehead in thought. What did, however, nearly knock Winston to the floor?

Rustler jump through the window of the bedroom where Winston was standing and all Winston could think at that moment was it wasn't like Rustler to jump up on him. It seemed Rustler was happy to see him home and yet, the moaning sound

AFTERMATH

Rustler made indicated that he was worried about something. "What is it, Rustler? Where's Joseph?"

Rustler immediately took command, leading Winston through the door of the kitchen to the outside. Trailing in behind Rustler, Winston immediately knew that even Rustler did not know where Joseph was. He knew this from the start as off the porch Rustler hit the ground with his nose down sniffing through the grass. So it was, Rustler only knew the whereabouts of Joseph, but was quickly picking up his scent and led Winston to the edge of the cornfield where Winston noticed a few corn stocks had been disturbed and was still bent over.

It became difficult to see which way Rustler went as it was clear he had homed in on what he was searching for. The rustling sound of the corn stalks was the only clue to where the dog was, and Winston strained a look over the tall corn stalks for a sign of Rustler's movement. Winston called out to his son, hoping just to hear his voice and know he was about. However, a few moments passed and no sound or sight of Joseph. It puzzled Winston as to why Joseph would be out here in the cornfield. True, the boy must have been fleeing from the house fire, but it seemed to make better sense to take to the barn or shed for shelter.

Winston could only wonder what led up to the house fire. It appeared a man had entered into the house from the front, met up with Rustler and all hell broke loose. The table lamp was knocked to the floor, smashed, and set the front part of the house ablaze. To escape the fire, Joseph must have made his way to the cornfield. Again Winston wondered why the cornfield and not the shed or barn?

Winston stopped a moment and listened out for the sounds of Rustler beating his way through the cornfield. Hardly a sound now, the stillness built an uneasy feeling in the pit of his stomach. Rustler had disappeared it seemed. With only a half hour before sunset Winston clamored his way out of the cornfield to a place where he could get a better view of his whereabouts. Desperate to find his son, he cupped his hands and raised them to his mouth, shouting his son's name.

Not far to the north Winston could see the access road and wondered if Joseph even made it this far on foot. The realization of what happened while he was away began to unfold before his eyes. Joseph had been chased by a second man to a place near the access road where a lone tree stood. In the dusk of the evening, he could see a figure of a young man hanging by the neck from that tree.

Winston's eyes widened, and his knees became weak. Someone had chased down his son Joseph and hanged him. Winston closed his eyes. Rustler would not have allowed this. But then, Rustler was unaware of this event as he was busy stripping out the throat of the man he saw at the door of his house.

CHAPTER 19

~Billy's Big Birthday Party~

Darby was up before daybreak. She hardly slept a wink thinking about all the things she and Auntie Edna had to prepare for Billy's birthday party. First, there had to be a happy birthday cake made and set out to cool while she and Auntie Edna made potholders as gifts for Billy. Darby helped stir the cake batter while Edna went about beating up some lard and powdered sugar for the icing. She arranged everything including a piping bag and tip and some food coloring she hadn't used in ages.

"Do you think Billy knows what we're doing?" Darby asked in a whisper while stealing glances at to Billy who was sitting in a chair at the table and acting innocently unaware.

Edna smiled and then replied, "I'm pretty sure he knows, but I'll bet he'll act surprised when we get ready to celebrate."

"How do you know?"

Edna put down her whisk and leaned over to whisper in Darby's ear. "I have a special surprise gift for him. I grow it behind the barn, and before Billy has a chance to figure out what it is, I cut off all the buds and let it seed. I then chop up the buds and put in a snap lid container and hide it in the cupboard!"

Even though Darby wasn't sure what it was Auntie Edna was talking about, she was thrilled just the same. She clenched her hands together, "Oh, Auntie Edna. This will be the best happy birthday ever!"

Darby giggled, and then put her hand over her mouth, "Oops," she said looking at Billy who was sitting across the table staring her way, "I mean we meant some other birthday party, Billy."

It was time to put the cake in the oven when Darby asked, "Does Billy have any friends? Maybe we can invite them over too."

"Well, honey. Yes, I think Billy does have friends, but mostly girlfriends. And I don't think it would be a good idea to invite them over because, well, Billy doesn't hide his feelings very well around his girlfriends."

Darby giggled, "You mean they do a lot of kissing?"

Edna's eyebrows raise, and she pursed her lips, after all, it was a tender subject, so she just gave Darby a nod yes.

"Billy's got a girlfriend; Billy's got a girlfriend ..."

It looked as if Billy didn't mind being teased by Darby. He just sat staring back at everyone. And Auntie Edna decided it was time to dig out the crayons and notebook paper and design a few sheets of Happy Birthday wrapping paper. Of

AFTERMATH

course, after that, it would be time to get the cake out of the oven to cool, and that meant it was time to make a few potholders.

Left alone to finish making wrapping paper, Edna Weatherly went to the sink to make up a pitcher of lemonade. While she was cutting and squeezing lemons, she looked up and out the window above the sink. Her eyebrows knitted and a smile turned to a frown at what she saw scurrying into the barn.

Sterling always kept a box of rat poison handy for getting rid of rats in the barn. And many times in the past she had to use the stuff, so she knew how to use it and use it well. Above the sink window out of the reach of children, she took down the box of poison rat pellets and dropped two of the pellets into an old stone mortar. She ground both the pellets into a fine powder with her mortar and pestle. She knew there was enough cyanide to kill a buffalo in just 1 pellet, but what the heck? Maybe two; one for each glass of lemonade would get the job done quicker.

"Marsha?"

"Yes Auntie Edna," Darby replied.

"How would you like some fresh squeezed lemonade?"

"Mmm, I love lemonade!"

* * *

~Mary~

~Late afternoon yesterday ...

She stood looking up at the thirty-foot-tall fiberglass lady. In the parking lot behind her, the old Oldsmobile had steam billowing out of the seams in the hood and out of the front grill. Mary Sawyer sighed; it was time to test out her new boots for walking. She thought to herself how being as tall as this statue, she would not fear a thing, and what's more, she could cover more ground in having a longer stride. Now that she had an additional 40 miles to cover meant a few more extra days away from her family.

Not that she complained or regretted finding herself in this situation; Mary wasn't sorry for having suffered this setback. She felt good having done what she did for Mel and his family. Mary simply could not imagine the anguish of Mel's family, not knowing what happened to him. What happened to Mel wasn't her fault she knew, but having the ability to provide Mel and his family closure was the right thing to do.

Gathering up her backpack and arrow, she gazed out to the southern horizon a moment. Out ahead her journey awaited, past the abandoned vehicles, some with their doors left open and some with smashed rear windows; the groups of buildings playing host to auditoriums of more abandoned vehicles nestled together; silent across the landscape. Only the very few, like this Oldsmobile, escaped the silent death that descended that day over a year ago, and now, it too has finally died. The world had become a hideous place of misfortune and terror at every turn. Everywhere Mary looked she saw the death of a society that once flourished. It was a place of security and warmth; where people laughed and smiled at one another and beckoned to strangers to have a nice day. Now, all that is left is strangers with gaunt faces and hollow cheeks where smiles forever are gone; eyes empty and without acknowledgment of anyone or anything.

Mary felt fortunate knowing she had a beautiful and prosperous family to come home to. The fact was, no matter what problems came their way; Winston would always come to the rescue. Mary thought of the many times she told Winston that is was nice to have a man around the house, and his reply would always be that is was equally nice to have a home with a 'woman's touch' to come home to. She could not imagine having found another man like Winston, and she knew in her heart that he was out searching for her right now. Hopefully, Darby was at home by now. No, she corrected herself, *Darby was home now*, and she could feel it. Winston would have found her by now and together with Joseph, they were all together out searching. And to think, if it had not been her escape from Dug and Justin, she'd be on a cargo ship headed to some strange land perhaps. Yes, it was true. Mary had heard them talk, even brag about their connections in Tampa, and how they were going to barter her off as a slave to some rich people in Europe somewhere.

Keeping her mind busy, Mary felt she was making better time in her travels along Tamiami Trail. Despite knowing she could walk anywhere along the medium or the road pavement if she desired, she kept close to one side of the road in case she had to scurry into the woods to hide. Even so, not even a bicycle let alone a car or truck had come down the road. In fact, she had not seen anyone at all. Remembering back a year ago, she recalled seeing people wandering around, seemingly in a daze. A few months after the skies flashed and things went dark, people began fighting one another. Soon after that, there were less and fewer people around. Even the roaming bands of hard cases started to thin out in numbers. Mary didn't want to dwell on what happened in Hartley. What happened to all the townspeople, whether most migrated to parts of the country to be with family or died, but now Hartley was a ghost town. It all seemed odd to Mary, how a town just barely five miles away from home, could suffer such an extreme misfortune without affecting her and Winston's life in the least.

The sun was just a few fingers from the horizon, casting long shadows from power poles and trees when Mary decided it was time to end her journey for the day. There was a campfire to make and water to boil, not to mention the warmth from the fire to help ease her to sleep. The two soda pop cans she carried in her pack, she filled from a ditch that had flooded from the past day's rain. The water ran clear, but she was deeply concerned about purifying it, so she went about looking for a spot in the woods far from the road and to where the wood was dry to build her campsite. The fire was essential for keeping animals from coming near, so she got started right away gathering plenty of wood for her fire. The disposable plastic lighter she found in the sporting goods store was a godsend, and before long Mary had a nice little fire going. She positioned her two soda pop cans in the fire using a hook-shaped twig she kept for the purpose of moving the cans in and out of the fire.

After the time spent boiling the water, Mary set them aside to cool down for the evening and then rummaged through her backpack for a naval orange she had acquired along with a ripe mango from a few roadside trees she passed along the way. It was always a habit for her to study the roadside fauna for anything bearing fruit, berries or nuts. "So far so good," she quietly said to herself. "Now if a fried fish would just jump out of that little creek over there, I'd be all set."

AFTERMATH

The next evening came, and in a camp 17 miles closer to home, she almost got her wish when she spied a big bullfrog jumping out of the little creek next to her camping spot. "Nice of you to come to dinner," she said to the bullfrog as she pinned him to the ground with a forked end of a branch she pulled from her little woodpile.

After a meal of navel orange, another ripe mango and nicely flame cooked frog's legs, Mary settled back wondering what a nice hot bath would feel like right about now. She was doing her best to keep her hair straight and untangling knots when she decided tomorrow before she broke camp, she would try to take a quick dip in the little stream nearby. She could use one of the tee-shirts she had gotten from the sporting goods store, or even her dress she had folded in the backpack to use as a towel. It would be nice to have soap, she thought.

It was not unusual this time of year for the overnight temperatures to fall into the low 60's, and with the high humidity, it felt even colder. Mary awoke from her bed of leaves she had mounded around her. The protection from small wisps of cold air and dew was a welcomed addition to her camping skills. It was contrary to the belief of her husband in that you should always spend the overnight sleeping as high off the forest ground as you can. As she sat up and leaned against a tree, she began to understand why. It seemed every flea in the forest had come to feast on her scalp. Even her eyebrows felt like they were moving. Instinctively, she grabbed up scraps of the orange peel she had tossed aside last night and rubbed the skins briskly through her hair and around her ears, and then her eyebrows until her entire face became sticky with the leftover orange essence. The citrus oil worked wonders.

Mary smiled in the thought of all the clever remedies and tonics she knew of. Being married to a Seminole Indian had its benefits as he had taught her many things; and Mary, being of Italian decent, fit together well with Winston's tribal friends; as most believed that she too, was of Seminole blood. However, having been born in Turin Italy to a family of humble farmers, Mary entered the convent to become a nun. She was only 22 at the time. The order of the Sacred Heart was known to be missionary nuns, and it wasn't long before traveling to the United States to join with patrons of her order to learn many things. Obedience, temperance and even learning to speak English and French were the main goals of the mission, which by this time had informed Mary that she would go on assignment in Haiti.

Having only served a few months in Haiti, she learned of the passing of her father in Turin, and that the family requested her home immediately for his funeral. Mary took leave from the mission and with little time to spare she left for Port-au-Prince on the first ship heading to Miami International Airport. Unfortunately, no ships left port that day, fearing rough unpassable seas. A hurricane was projected to land by nightfall and as desperate as Mary was to attend her father's funeral, she hired a pilot to fly her to Miami International Airport. However, there was something wrong with the plane's registration numbers, and she was flown to a private airstrip near Brown Dairy Road instead. With no money left for a cab, Mary began walking the 10 or so miles to the airport, hoping at least to wire home for plane fare.

Mary recalled how the winds began picking up, and before she left the airstrip for the road, she felt the sting of the rain beating against her face. She recalled the pilot saying that he'd never experience a tailwind like this one. He laughed saying he could literally fly the plane here with the engine turned off. Mary wasn't one to believe such nonsense as that, but now as she tried to make her way to the airport, she had begun to wonder if in fact she would make it or be swept up in the approaching cyclone.

T.A. Walters

As Mary recalled, that whole day came into focus in her mind; it was a day that changed her life. The rustling noise of her habit blowing in the wind drowned out the horns of passing cars headed west on Brown Dairy Road. She gripped the shawl around her shoulders tightly hoping to stave off the bitter cold sting of the rain, but she was dressed in the tropical habit of fine light woven linen, and she began to shiver uncontrollably.

Finally, a pickup truck swung over from the westbound lane and stopped, blocking her path on the roadside. She stared back at him as she slowly hobbled the uneven shoulder of the road to get around him.

Mary heard the truck door slam shut and then seconds later two strong arms cradled her shoulders, "Please do not be afraid," he told her while leading her to his truck and helping her in.

Long ago in school, she had learned that the words, 'be not afraid' were the first words of an angel to someone in need. And it was soon after, she found herself a friend in Winston. He told her of all she needed to know on the way home, and that he had been released early from the dealership where he worked as a car mechanic. And that the reason there was only westbound traffic was that there were evacuation orders for Miami because of the approaching hurricane. "Looks like you were going in the wrong direction!" he exclaimed. He also told her no planes were heading in or out of the airport, and she would be safe waiting out the storm at his grandfather's house.

The hurricane came taking with it part of the roof and his grandfather's spirit as Winston would say. Mary knew he died suddenly of a heart attack, but fortunately, she had the pleasure of meeting him and talking to him about life in general. He spoke in great lengths of how life formed a big circle and how things that should be, unfortunately, does not happen well within that circle. He hoped that Winston would find the right woman and raise up a family.

Mary smiled. Her father felt the same way. Odd how it came to be that Winston would lose his grandfather and her father all in a matter of a few days. It was as if the grandfather was speaking the final words of her father from halfway around the world.

The very next day, the skies cleared and Winston was on the roof repairing and rebuilding their life together. From that day, Mary never looked back.

Life happens for a reason, and Mary found the true meaning in her life.

AFTERMATH

CHAPTER 20

~A Birthday Party with a cake, lemonade, and death~

Edna poured two glasses of lemonade for her and Darby. She set the drinks down on the table, "I think a little lemonade would be nice, don't you think?" Darby shook her head and smiled. She told her Auntie Edna she made the best lemonade ever! Of course, her mother made some pretty good lemonade, but Auntie Edna's lemonade was special.
    Edna went back to the kitchen sink to make some paste out of flour and water. Since the kitchen and table were part of the front room, she was never out of sight of Darby at the table. "You cut some strips out of the paper okay honey, and I'll make us up some paste to make a nice long paper chain to hang down from the ceiling!"
    Darby was enjoying her lemonade while working to make decorations for the big party. Edna licked some of the flour paste from her fingers, "Yum," she said. "You know Marsha, you can eat my paste, and it won't hurt you. But it is pretty bland, kind of sour you might say."
    Edna and Darby went about pasting the paper chain together with their fingers and alternating licks with each link to clean little fingertips. They laughed together because making a Happy Birthday Party was so much fun!
    However, just now a bad man kicked the front door open and stood in the doorway looking around. He was carrying a rifle, and behind him, a lady with lots of tattoos stood by; her eyes were red like as if she'd been crying, but a silly grin covered her face instead.
    "Make a move, and I'll blow your head off – and that goes for the kid too!" exclaimed the bad man
    "Oh, but of course," Edna replied. "We've been expecting you, folks."
    The man's eyes scrunched up like the drawstrings of a lady's purse. "Whaa?"
    Darby sang out, "We're having a birthday party!"
    The man looked around, "Oh yeah, where's the cake?"
    The woman behind the man turned her head to look inside. "I can use some cake right about now."
    "Well come right in and sit down," Edna begged. "The cake is in the oven and won't take long before it's done."
    "But Auntie Edna, we don't want to eat the cake until it's made pretty and it's time to blow out the candles."
    The bad lady spoke, "You know it does smell real good."

"Shut up," the rifleman said to his lady friend. "Just go in the bedroom and grab some pillowcases so we can load up some grub and anything else worth taking."

"Easy you dumass," she said. "I was figuring we'd just take this place as our own."

Edna interrupted, "There there, don't be arguing. And above all no cussing in front of the child! You two friends be seated, and I'll go check on the cake."

The rifleman snapped his rifle up and took aim on Edna, "You just do that, and if you make any suspicious moves I'll blow your head off!"

"Chrissakes, Jimmy, we're taking the house. Just shoot them both right now!"

"Not in the house, Heather! I ain't putting up with the mess. We'll take care of it outside."

Edna huffed, "Do you want me to check the cake or not?"

"Auntie Edna, are they really gonna shoot us?"

"No honey, just keep working. Everything is going to be alright," Edna said turning a glance back at the table where Darby sat, tears welling up in her eyes. Turning back to look at the rifleman she continued, "Now let me make this perfectly clear – while in *this* house, we respect one another."

"Yeah," said Heather, "What we do to one another outside the house is another."

Edna poked her finger on the cake. It wasn't quite done. "It's going to be a few minutes," she told the two desperados. "Why don't you both sit down at the table with us and enjoy a freshly squeezed glass of lemonade while you wait?"

The rifleman grinned, "While now you're talking, that'll be great what do you think Heather?"

Heather sat down with her boyfriend and then slapped his thigh as she leaned into him and whispered in his ear, "That old chick is a crazy bitch, eh?"

"I don't know about that, she reminds me a little of my grandmother."

Edna retrieved the two glasses of lemonade she made special for those two rats when she saw them prowling around her barn earlier. She was setting them down in front of them when she overheard Heather tell her boyfriend Jimmy not to worry, and that she would handle the old lady and put her down humanely.

Edna smiled as she watched both Heather and Jimmy chug the entire contents of the cyanide-laced lemonade. It went very quick indeed. Heather's eyes crossed moments before her head slammed down on the table. On the other hand, Jimmy fought off the effects of the cyanide, but only long enough to say he thought Heather had been poisoned.

"You too, you dumb ox!"

Of course, Edna wasted no time dragging them out and onto the porch. The rifle she kicked under the davenport with other guns, several in fact. It wasn't that she hated firearms, no – it was just she liked having them handy in places no one would ever expect.

A little while later, and after Edna took the cake out of the oven to cool, Darby went to the front door to ask Auntie Edna if it was okay to wrap some of Billy's gifts before the paste dried up in the bowl. She had to yell over the sound of the tractor motor as Auntie Edna was busy dragging those two bad people away with ropes tied behind the tractor.

Edna yelled back her reply. "Yes honey, go ahead. Auntie Edna will be right back in a jiffy!"

AFTERMATH

*　*　*

~Mary~

For Mary Sawyer, there was no debating in her mind, the issue over whether to jump into the cold waters of the small creek nearby. She felt it was best to wash up in the evening when the heat of the day and her walking had warmed her up. Getting back on the road was the most important thing on her mind now. The more time spent during the daylight hours walking, the more distance she could cover. So without further thought, she strapped on her backpack and headed out of the woods to resume her trek home.

Random thoughts filled her mind as she walked along Tamiami Trail. Thoughts of having killed two men and whether she would suffer through eternity for having done such troubled her. It was enough to know that killing was against God's laws as it was written in the Ten Commandments. She knew that in the past many a good man's faith had been tested, and she wondered if she were being tested by God. How could one be tested over the love of her family ... her children? How could striking back at evil be punishable? Mary knew it was not for her to judge or decide, but rather to offer up that decision to God's wisdom. He and only he could offer the guidance to make it through difficult times.

Would it not be selfish of her to spare her own life for the lives of her loved ones? It angered Mary to think that way, but she could not see nor rationalize it in any other way. It was her duty as a wife and mother to protect her and her children in any way possible. And she did just that.

A passing car heading in the opposite direction broke Mary from her thoughts. As the car passed, she noticed there were two people in the car. A white-haired man and a woman of around the same age, who it seemed, did not see her. It lifted her spirits in the thought that she didn't appear as a person of any particular interest. Having her hair tucked under her hat and pulled down low gave the appearance that she was an impecunious male traveler. Her baggy camouflaged shirt and pants also helped in disguising her as a woman. Mary smiled, impecunious indeed!

Scrubby, impecunious men drift to and fro there, waiting for the gods to provide something easy; and the prudent man, conscious of the possession of loose change, whizzes through the danger zone at his best speed, 'like one that on a lonesome road doth walk in fear and dread, and having once turned round walks on, and turns no more his head, because he knows a frightful fiend doth close behind ...

In all such fear, Mary hoped for; was to be left alone to complete her journey back home, and with only 60 miles or less, she figured she'd be there in as little as 3 days. But she had to keep moving. Her goal was to cover at least 20 miles from sunup to sundown. Carrying with her was her trusty arrow which she idly swept at the tall grass along the roadside while she ambled on. The arrow reminded her of the times her and Winston would steal away on camping trips before the children were born. Many times Winston would set up a dinner campfire to cook a meal of rabbit, squirrel, or fish using an arrow as a spit for a rotisserie setup to hang and turn the meat over the fire.

It was already noon, and Mary felt the pangs of hunger. Thinking of food and dinner campfires didn't help matters, so instead, she took out her little soda can of water and drank a few sips. She didn't want to slow down now, especially during the most productive part of the day's journey home. After all, she had a home waiting for her return and was not inclined to make the outdoors her place of living. It reminded her of how sometimes she had to wander into the woods to find Joseph so she could coax him home as a child. It would be dinnertime and dark soon, and as she recalled many times finding Joseph busy trying to build a fire by rubbing sticks together. He'd always had something ready to cook. Most of the time a fish or a frog or two and that surprised Mary. Joseph was only 5 years old at the time, and he would cry as she dragged him home all the while he sobbed about wanting to live out the rest of his life in the woods. Joseph was so much like his father and would copy everything his father did, right down to the way Winston walked when he was feeling proud. Joseph and Winston would swagger along making up things to say about how each one was the greatest hunter or warrior in the land. Mary laughed thinking how many times the two would sneak up to scare her while she quietly hung up clothes on the clothesline. Her mind would be focused on the essential things of the day like what to cook for dinner, or how Darby was making out, dressing her little straw doll on the porch swing.

Mary's thoughts were interrupted by the sound of movement in the thick brush along the roadside. She paused a moment, stopping to study the area from which the noise came. It was a combination of things she heard; the rustle of tall grass and the crackle of dried leaves and brush. While her eyes followed the direction and sound coming from the woods, she saw nothing. The idea that whatever it was that made the noises had to be short enough not to be seen. Mary had become confident that it may be a curious animal such as a raccoon or maybe some squirrels scurrying from one place to another.

After an hour of walking along the edge of the forest, the noise followed. Mary tried picking up the pace by running in short bursts, covering perhaps a few hundred yards at a time. Even so, the creature in the woods would catch up to her and continue following her. The rustle in the woods seemed to become more pronounced, however, and Mary was beginning to believe there were more than just one animal following along. The thought formed in her mind that she was being tracked by a

AFTERMATH

larger animal than just a raccoon. Mary rummaged through her backpack for her 38 special revolver. She had checked the pistol earlier to make sure it was loaded but stopped to recheck it to make sure. The confidence gained made all the difference in the world to Mary, but she decided to cross the highway and walk on the other side of the road.

Chapter 21

~Mary takes a stand~

Mary had counted 7 vehicles the whole day long, and none of those vehicles bothered to stop, and that was a good thing. So now with the sun only a fist above the horizon and a bath desperately needed, Mary felt she had an appointment with setting up a campsite about now. As bad luck would have it, there was no water to be found. Venturing deeper and deeper into the woods, she finally came upon a swampy area with tall standing grass, reeds, and cattails emerging through the standing water. Her instincts told her, despite it being daylight still; she should take the time to build a fire first. But she was eager to wash off the sweat and grime from her body, so at once she disrobed, hanging her shirt and pants on a nearby tree branch.

She slipped into the warm water of the shallow pond letting her head briefly dip below the surface. Shuffling her fingertips along her scalp, she re-dipped her head again bringing about fond memories of Sunday morning baths down at the gator hole. The gator hole was a spring-fed pond not more than a few hundred steps down the garden path from the house. It was also the fishing hole where small bluegill fish swam in abundance. Winston called them pan fryers and would often bring home dozens of them for Sunday dinner out on the picnic table by the barn and banana plants. He would fry up some hush puppies just in case the kids got a fishbone stuck in their throats.

Mary softly laughed with the memory of little Darby freaking out over having a fishbone stuck in her throat and Winston cramming a small hush puppy in her mouth and ordering her to chew it up and swallow it. The look on Darby's face was priceless when she found the fishbone had disappeared to her belly. It since dawned on Mary that Winston never served fish without having bread on the table, but hush puppies were the best he would always say. Like swallowing a scouring pad, he joked.

Her mind buried in the fond memories of the past, the rustle of ground debris jarred her back to the moment at hand. She sat still and silent, not wanting to make the slightest ripple in the water much less the tiniest splash.

A long moment of time passed.

It seemed like several minutes, even more now that she could hear just the sound of her own breathing. There was no sound around her, and now she wondered if she had also listened to the sound of something out there. Mary slowly rose to her feet and moved to the tree where her clothes hung from the lower branch of a big oak tree. She had a clean shirt tucked inside her backpack but opted to use the one she had worn for the last day or so. Her backpack, more than a few steps away, seemed too far to fetch at the moment.

Mary had just finished zippering up her pants when she heard a loud rustle in the forest behind her, and then another in the area just off to the right. From about a distance of only 40 or 50 yards behind the oak tree, the forest opened up with the thrashing sound of a pack of hungry dogs heading her way in a full run. Leaping through a small clearing of tall grass, the dogs lurched; their backs arched and visible enough to appear as an enormous side-winder in the mire.

Her body in rhythm with her heart leaped, grasping for the purchase of an overhead oak branch that could provide safe refuge from the attacking pack of dogs. Pulling herself up she hooked a leg over the branch and continued her climb grabbing hold of another branch higher up. She felt the fur and the hot breath of the first dog to reach her as it swept past her foot. Had it not been for the spacing of these big trees boughs it would have been over for her she knew, as she climbed higher to a fork in the branches that she made for her a safe and somewhat comfortable place to sit.

* * *

Darby was in tears by the time Aunt Edna put away the tractor and entered the house. It was necessary to deliver the guests to a resting spot far away from home. Times being what they were, taking chances with filth results in serious health issues for the living. Besides, there were plenty of hungry forest friends who would take care of the remnants of abandoned corpses. The idea that Darby was scared because Auntie Edna had been so long in taking care of those two indigents, but it wasn't that, that troubled Darby after all.

"Auntie Edna," Darby cried. "Billy left the house, and I don't know when he'll be back."

Edna moved to cradle Darby's head in her arms, "Oh honey don't worry, he'll be back home in a little while."

"But how do you know Auntie Edna?"

"He always does when he's hungry, and that won't be long from now. Why-I suspect, he'll be home right about now!"

Edna pointed to the direction of the window. "You see, yonder comes Billy now."

Darby reached up and hugged Edna's neck. Edna heard Darby sniff and knew she was crying.

"What's a matter, Marsha? Billy's home now, don't cry."

"But Auntie Edna, Billy came home ... and I am so far away from home."

Edna looked at Darby with a patronizing frown, and then smiled brightly saying, "I don't think you should worry about that. I will see to it that you get home myself!"

Darby began clapping her little hands and then smiled brightly in return. "You will?"

"Why of course dear-heart. I will take you home myself."

"Can we go on the next happy day?"

"Of course!"

Billy's Birthday Party was a smashing success, even though he didn't really care for the taste of the cake. He did, however, love his potholders, and the gift of Catnip Edna had given him wrapped up in an old sock. When it comes to Catnip as all cats know, including Billy, it was best after a good meal of shredded chicken.

Darby giggled to see Billy roll around on the floor with his sock of Catnip. "Once he sleeps this one off," Edna told Darby. "He'll be as spunky as a kitten. So don't be surprised if you wake up with Billy in your bed."

"I love Billy, he's so funny," Darby mused.

"He loves you too honey."

"Can he sleep over at my house?"

"We'll see. Now let's go off to bed, and I tuck you in and read you the story of Goldilocks and the Three Bears."

Auntie Edna found that was Darby's favorite story and she never got tired of having it read to her. So Edna lit a couple of lamps as now it was beginning to get dark outside the house and led Darby off to bed.

* * *

~Mary~

The idea that the pack of wild dogs would give up and move on was wishful thinking on Mary's part. Mary counted 4 dogs, and the same 4 dogs hung around long after the sun dipped below the horizon. All she could think of now was that revolver she had packed away in her backpack that hung from the branch of a nearby tree. If there were any chance of her to retrieving that gun, it would have to come with the hope that she could figure out a way to transfer herself over to that tree from this one. But then, she would have to go low enough to reach the backpack which would place her within reach of the largest dog.

AFTERMATH

If only I had built a fire; and if I had just hung my backpack on this tree.

She realized that this could be the end. Judging by the persistence of these hungry animals, she would not get out of this alive. All 4 starving animals, their ribcage bones showing and their tongues lapping out over hungry mouths told her she would eventually become weak from hunger, thirst, and lack of sleep. All this would come soon she knew.

Despite the hunger and her thirst, she went to work thinking about how she might safely get a little bit of sleep. She had nothing on her that she could use to strap herself to the tree as a safety harness to ensure she didn't fall out onto the ground. However, it was a certainty she wouldn't get much sleep tonight. The best she could come up with was to loop one arm around a branch above her while she leaned against the trunk of the tree. Obvious that her arm would eventually fall asleep bothered her not. It would be a good wake-up call to reinforce her position in the tree and thus ensure she could keep tabs on the activity on the ground. It was 'wishful' thinking on her part to think these starving beasts would lay-off a chance for a meal. Maybe sleep is what she thought may make a difference in clearing her mind until she could come up with a plan of escape, or better still, a way to retrieve her gun.

Chapter 22

~Death was her only way out~

Having spent the evening in a tree, Mary was exhausted, hungry and thirsty. Her hearing became acute as she could hear the tongues of those stubborn carnivores lapping water from the place she had bathed the evening before. It was now less than an hour until sunset of the second day she had spent in boughs of the mighty oak tree. And as the sun was setting, she looked up at the darkening sky through the branches that made up the canopy above her.

There just a few yards above her head was a dark object. It was large and held in place by a few branches that strained to secure it in place; branches that bowed under the massive weight of an object that appeared as if it waited for the perfect time. The time to fall, Mary certainly knew, and that object was what it was: deadfall. *Great! Death above me and death below.* With an object as large as this suspended chunk of a tree limb, one could easily see it would crush anything up to the size of a school bus.

Mary knew the best place to be was above this deadfall and not below it as she was now, so she took what bit of energy she had left in her to climb up higher and higher until she was able to squeeze around the half rotten tree limb to a spot just above. Thirty feet below her lay a ring of sleeping dogs huddled tightly around the base of the oak tree she was trapped in. *If I can dislodge this deadfall and make it drop on that nest of dogs, this alone would be better than I hoped for.*

Sending up a prayer she positioned her feet on the old log while hanging tight to the limb near her face. If there was a chance the old bough cut loose and fell, she needed to know she would remain up here and not riding the down with the deadfall. Holding on tight Mary jumped up and down on the giant log with each attempt making a loud snapping noise – *two, three, four ...* she counted. Then all at once on the fifth jump, the log cut loose and slid straight down along the length of the tree and impaled at least one of the beasts. A horrific sound of yelps and frightened groans split the night in agony.

Later as Mary was finding the best way to get comfortable, she heard the scramble of dog feet and snorting sounds muffled in what she knew were hungry survivors feasting on the dead.

A pale halo of the yellow sun began a new day over the horizon. Mary awoke with a sudden jerk. The whereabouts of her position slowly came to her along with a painful stiffness in her neck. She shuffled her hands up and down her arms trying to ward off the chill and yawned while wondering how long it would be before the dogs

AFTERMATH

gave up and moved away. She knew she at least threw a scare into them last night with the dropping of the deadfall log. However now, it seemed so quiet down below, and she strained to see clearly whatever advantage she might have gained.

Mary stretched her aching muscles and rubbed the life back into her thighs and lower legs before attempting to lower herself down the tree. From a level where she had first settled before climbing higher the day before, Mary could not discern whether the dogs were about or not. There indeed was no sound down there. She thought about waiting until the sun was completely up, but being as quiet as it was, she felt the animals may still be asleep. Perhaps this would be her only chance at getting her gun before all hell breaks loose. She could survive a certain number of dog bites, but depending on where those bites landed would determine if she would survive the attack before getting the chance to defend herself.

She looked across to the tree beside her and the backpack that hung from a limb on that tree. Mary knew she could have that gun in her hand in less than 15 seconds once her feet hit the ground. With having the surprise advantage over the dogs, she felt she had at least 5 to 8 seconds of that time in her favor. Mary knew she could hang out on her perch awhile waiting for the sun to fully rise, but what advantage would that serve? If anything, it would only help to give the beasts time to wake up and stretch.

Mary took in a deep breath, dropped to the ground and dashed over to her backpack. The zippered pouch where her gun was, took the longest time to open. Mary struggled with the zipper. It was stuck, jammed closed. Having made several quick attempts to unstick the zipper with no success, she quickly snapped her backpack free of the limb and slung the pack over her shoulder. Expecting to have dogs biting on her heels, she scurried back up the tree to the place she was before. Out of breath and gasping for air, Mary tugged and pulled on the stuck zipper while struggling to keep from falling out her makeshift tree stand.

She worked in the quiet envelope of silence that surrounded her when the realization that the dogs had gone away. The sun had begun filtering passed the trees casting with it long misty shafts of light through the forest. Mary stopped and gazed down below to the forest floor. Patches of dog fur were all about, and remnants of the ripped up animal was nearby the base of the tree along with the big log that she had dropped last night. Small branches and leaves were strewn all over the ground, and a short distance away was the mangled remnant of one dog.

Mary gasped at the sight of her own feet, for them both were covered in blood. She had run through a slew of dog remnants, and it repulsed her to know she would have to walk through bloody entrails once she dropped down from her tree stand. Busying her mind with the zippered pocket on her backpack she discovered in the new light of the day, a sewing thread had gotten caught up in the zipper. With the thread in one hand and the zipper in the other, she worked it free and opened up her gun pouch. Sliding the pistol into her pants pocket, she swore to herself that she and this gun would never part company again. In fact, she would make it an extension of her hand wherever she went.

At this point in her travels, Mary thought of herself a novice with much to learn about making the cut on her own. Being in the wilderness and on the road, she knew that all senses needed to remain at attention. It didn't mean she had to dedicate her thinking along that narrow avenue of thought of course, but it did mean always being alert to everything around oneself. Nonetheless, she felt she was doing reasonably well so far. That is if she didn't starve or dehydrate herself first, which brought about one important thought – get a fire going and purify some drinking water.

Getting out of the tree this time was a bit tricky in that the idea there was no way to avoid the grisly after-matter that cluttered the ground. She told herself to suck it up and go with it, but mental rehearsals never go to plan.

The first things she did when her feet hit the ground were slip and fall. It was enough to make a bull stag puke. But Mary managed to pull herself together and race to the small pond and wash off – clothes and all. The gun, she kept close by on the dry bank next to her. When she was convinced she had washed off all the bloody mess from her clothes and her feet were clean, she returned to fetch the two soda cans she kept handy as drink containers. Also, getting her boots back on her feet was a priority; however, it appeared the dogs taken off with her boots.

She quickly resigned to the fact that she'd be trekking home barefoot, and she turned her attention to setting up a campfire. At least sometime throughout the day, she felt relieved in the thought that her clothes would begin to dry nicely before the next sunset. The fire was of great help, and it felt nice and warm as the muscles relaxed from the early morning chill. Hypnotized by the dancing flames, she thought about getting home and at last bathing and getting into nice clean clothes. Cooking for Winston and the children filled her mind with the thought that Darby should have made it home safely. After all, it was only about a mile or so straight down the road from town.

Mary's eyes grew dark and her eyebrows lowered, *I did tell Darby which way to go.*

Mary closed her eyes tight and leaned back her head in thought. She tried to recollect if she had made Darby aware of which way to go. Mary was almost sure Darby knew the road home and in any case ... *no, I didn't tell her which way to go!* It was at the moment of being trapped in the laundromat bathroom she told Darby to go the opposite direction into town to the church. She recalled now, telling Darby to get Brother Jonas to go help her find her father. Realizing now, Darby was all alone because Brother Jonas was seriously shot.

Sniffing back tears, she tried to rub-away the worry and fear from her face. *Oh, Father in Heaven ...* she began to pray, *help guide my baby home.*

AFTERMATH

* * *

~Auntie Edna and Darby pack the tractor for the ride home~

Edna was tying down a picnic lunch over the rear hitch of the tractor while Darby stood by asking questions.

"Don't you think we should take Billy with us, Auntie Edna?"

She smiled back at Darby, "No, he doesn't like riding on the tractor, although I have had Billy ride once or twice before, he gets hard to handle, and I have to hold him by the scruff of his neck all the way home while I steer with one hand."

Darby frowned and then pointed over toward the barn at a dusty Cadillac park beside it. It had green mold growing on the windows here and there. "Why can't we take the car and then Billy can ride inside?"

"Honey," said Edna, "that car doesn't run anymore. Besides, riding on the tractor is fun, don't you think? And don't you worry about Billy. He'll hang out in the house and sleep all day. I left him plenty to eat and a clean litter pan."

"But Auntie Edna, he'll be lonely."

Edna climbed up and sat behind the wheel, then hoisted Darby into her lap. "No. Billy will watch TV."

"I thought the TV doesn't work."

"When Billy's awake he stares a lot and sometimes he stares at the TV set. I guess he makes believe he's watching a kitty show."

Edna twisted the key to start the tractor, but after a few attempts it tried to start, but the diesel engine sputtered then stopped. "Drat!" Edna exclaimed. "This tractor is hard to start; especially in the morning."

"Can you mend it?"

"Sure can honey; stand up and let Auntie Edna down. You see Marsha, the pre-heater whatchamacallit-its are broke, and Sterling was gonna fix it, but he went to heaven before he got the chance to." Edna chuckled, "Sterling would always say the only thing colder than me was this here old tractor!"

"Poor poor tractor," Darby said sympathetically.

Edna reached behind the seat and grabbed a yellow self-igniting bottle-torch and then got down and went to one side of the tractor motor. She popped the trigger on the torch, and it lit right up with the roar of a small jet engine. Darby watched intently as Auntie Edna fanned big blue flame over the engine manifold. A few minutes later Edna was back behind the wheel starting the engine. Just like magic, the engine came to life, and Darby clapped her hands in delight. At last, she was going home.

Chapter 23

~Mary travels a stretch of treachery~

The sun had reached overhead, and Mary figured she had traveled 3 or more miles. Barefooted but in the soft grasses of the road shoulder, she marveled at the sight of one of her boots lying mangled in the grass. It was too chewed up to wear, but the idea she was heading in the direction of the wild dog pack began to trouble her mind. The best thing in her favor she knew was that she was behind them and as luck would have it, she was downwind of their position.

With that and the confidence that she was clear of danger, for now, she happened along a long stretch of orange trees ripe with navel oranges. It was the 'Cadillac' of the orange family as far as she was concerned. She didn't have to go into the grove far to fetch down three nice ones, double the size of her fist. There were two for her backpack and one to eat along the way. However, there was something about these trees that came familiar to her.

It was some time ago, long before the world dove into despair and everything was right in life, that this was a truck farm bustling with fruit pickers and row houses. There was a big equipment barn filled with tractors and crop sprayers and such. As she passed the access road down to the farm, she could see the old homestead of barns and row houses and how overgrown they'd become. It was like a mini ghost town now. Her heart ached of all the things that had just gone away. The memories that seemed so long ago, but was far more than a few years now drew sadness in her. Those times when the children would follow behind her in the garden while she gathered ripe vegetables and they would pick peas and shell the pods right there and eat the peas, so crisp and sweet. Of how they would brag about how their daddy showed them how to get those peas to eat in the garden, warmed her heart with pride.

Things change, and the world evolved, but never the children she begrudgingly thought. Those memories at least would remain in her heart for all times. They were like photographs in her mind, just like this old truck farm and the places she recalled along the way. The only thing that changes – no she thought, the change was not to be; it came for only the electric that turned people to the lives they chose and the chaos that followed when it was forever gone …

Above the power transformer hung from a tall pole, with its cables and veins of circulation that spread across the land, now remained silent; no buzzing noise no nothing, just the quiet that God gave the world. The sound of the wind in the boughs and the birds that sing their sweet refrain of the morning past, gave Mary the solace to continue, warm in the thought that soon the security of her family awaited her over the next horizon.

AFTERMATH

These were the thoughts that ran like an old filmstrip in Mary's mind. Not long after she had begun spending time with Winston, she recalled the day they drove up to Duval Canal. There was a long and dusty road that ran 30 miles through the wilderness and pasture lands that led to the secret fishing spot that Winston loved. The road came to a dead end where stood an old mailbox and what appeared a seldom traveled extension to the road, all overgrown with grass, but the way was clear to Winston as Mary recalled. Winston stopped for an old woman who sauntered slowly up to the window on Winston's side of the truck. She placed her hands on the sill of Winston's window sill, and Mary could still recall as if it were yesterday of how the 97-year-old woman stopped to chat with Winston. She talked about the old days when she and her great-grandfather would sit and sing on the porch of an old house a short distance away, behind her. She was just a little girl then, and her great-grandfather talked about things of past that he experienced. She mentioned that at that time, her great-grandfather was about 80 or so years old; and she seemed so proud of the stories he told that she didn't want Winston and her to leave until she talked about all the many memories she had growing up with her great-grandfather.

One of the most striking things she remembered this old woman was her telling Winston was of how her great-grandfather had enlisted in the Southern Army during the Civil War early on and how he had followed General Lee to the end of the war, all the way to where he fought on the battlefield at Gettysburg Pennsylvania. Her great-grandfather fought, she said to protect her homeland from those who wanted to take all that away. It was ever since then the sugar plantation never fell into enemy hands and thus gave her the luxury of never having to leave her home.

Mary was surprised that the old woman told her and Winston she had never left this place so much as traveled the road beyond a mile or so. At the time it didn't really make much of an impact on Mary; those words she had heard the old lady say. But now, a tear ran down her cheek in the thought of how she cherished the values that the old lady felt. People back then were indeed not really that much different than those today. It was just we've been masked by a mirage of artificial forces in our lives. Mary felt she had been blessed with the honor of having had such an experience as this, while at the same time thoughts of her own humble beginnings came to roost.

Looking back, she had the best of all education had to offer her; having attended Universities from Toulouse France to Turin Italy, taking residence in the convent of sisterhood, Mary studied the disciplines in Theology and finally at the age of 22 a nun in the order of the Sacred Heart. She was 26 when she left the convent to marry Winston. Now 38, Mary has no regrets.

Mary was happy and well suited in the life she lived today. Having been raised an only child on a goat farm, she had been one of a few lucky children who was bestowed the philanthropist's hearts that recognized her academic skills and devotion to the church. However, following the day she met Winston was the day she fell off the earth for those who knew her; in the sense that, she quietly walked away from her past life and began her new life with the man she loved.

There was no one and nothing in her life now that mattered to her more than that day forward when she and Winston became man and wife and started a family. Winston completed her life and gave her more than all the wealth in the world could possibly give. He gave her meaning and such beautiful children to cherish in her old age.

Mary walked along keeping a wandering eye on her surroundings and casually whipping the tall grass with her arrow. There were many times she had adjusted her course as there were many dead automobiles and trucks in her path. Some of those vehicles had caught fire and burned long ago. There were even a few motorcycles left lying in the tall grass, abandoned as if the rider simply lost interest and let the motorcycle drop where it died. Mary chuckled at the sight of one burned-out car with the pine tree deodorant still hanging from the rearview mirror. For whatever reason, the cardboard pine tree didn't burn and fall to the dash. And then there was the occasional burned out vehicle with the ghostly remnants of their occupants left inside. Mary would grimace and quickly look away.

However, as she looked away, she caught a glimpse of a young girl clutching flowers and kneeling down alongside a burned-out vehicle. She seemed focused on the act of carefully arranging those flowers so that she never seemed to notice when Mary walked up. Clearing her throat didn't arouse any attention her way, and as Mary stood over the young girl, she noticed a strange looking tattoo on the girl's forearm.

"Those are lovely," Mary began. "Daisies and Morning Glories?"

The girl looked over her shoulder and up at Mary. She gently brushed a lock of golden hair from her face. "We grow them."

Nothing unusual in that Mary became curious about where 'we' lived. They seemed far away from anything that she began to wonder where this girl lived.

"My name's Mary. Do you live nearby?"

A frightened expression suddenly marked her face as her eyes shifted back and forth. "You must leave. Leave now!"

Mary detected an urgency the young woman's voice, and it made her skin crawl. There didn't seem to be anyone around in either direction and what caused the alarm in this girl was not apparent, unless someone lay wait in the forest nearby the road shoulder.

AFTERMATH

The movement of the air seemed to stop, and the feeling that someone was watching not far into the forest crept over her as she felt as if she'd become enclosed in a vacuum.

Slightly bending forward to whisper in the girl's ear as she knelt in the grass, Mary asked, "Are we being watched?"

The girl didn't say but merely gave her head a few short nods. Mary asked, "From the forest behind us?"

"There are two," the girl replied. "Be on your way ... quickly."

She gently placed her hand on the girl's forearm and felt her tremble slightly. "Are you in trouble?"

"Their coming, go!"

"Come with me," Mary urged. "I'll protect you."

Much to Mary's surprise, the young girl jumped to her feet and grabbed hands, and they both ran as fast as they could until the sound of footfall overtook them. Mary dodged hard to the right, and they both ran into the forest. Something hard and sharp jabbed the sole of Mary's left foot, and she let out a short yelp as she tumbled to the ground in pain. For a moment she writhed in pain, but soon found she had stepped on a dead branch and that she suffered only minor bruising. The young girl was beginning to panic and tugged at Mary's arm, "We have to go hide!"

Hobbling to her feet, she limped along as fast as she could until they came to a section of Cyprus trees. Surrounding a dozen or so 100-year-old Cyprus trees were dozens of Cyprus knees of various stages of growth. Some as short a foot tall, others as tall as 4 and 5 feet tall. Getting lost in this stand of Cyprus trees wasn't hard, but getting invisible amongst the Cyprus knees was more natural, especially with the many old broken tree boughs lying about.

Mary and the young girl burrowed in between a cluster of knees and dragging over them, a bough of branches and leaves. From within, she could see the tall shadows of two men lurking about, stopping and then moving along in short distances nearby. What Mary could make out, was both men armed with clubs or bats, had not shaven or bathed in a while. They were both thin, and they both would pause and stand quietly for a moment. She could hear them sniffing the air like a pair of hounds and at one point turned as if they were about to leave or change direction until one stopped and motioned to the other of something that interested them. It appeared to be something in Mary and the young girl's direction. Mary then realized her foot was exposed, and she slowly retracted that foot, bringing her knee close to her chin.

Mary's mind raced with the idea of a plan of escape. Surely these cavemen would give up and turn away, she thought; but if they didn't what then? What relationship did this sweet young lady have with these brutish individuals? Now was not the time to discuss such things, and Mary knew that this may be a situation that may require deadly force. She had her pistol, but it wasn't as handy as it should have been. True, she had it on her, but it was behind her in her backpack, and now, the two men were drawing so close she and the young girl held their breath. Mary knew she was pretty well concealed from view because of the camouflaged pants and black shirt she wore, but the young girl in a white dress could be easily spotted through the spaces between branches. Lying in behind Mary, the young girl was nearly concealed from view, but her heavy breathing was not.

Mary felt the pressure of the cover branches on her as one of the men poked the area of her concealment with a baseball bat. She could see him quite well, but as the expression on his face, it was apparent he didn't spot her.

Yet.

Chapter 24

~*Darby's Journey Home*~

Had it been the day before, Darby may have spotted her daddy's pickup truck passing along the road she and Auntie Edna traveled now. But Winston was a day out and determined to find her and her mother. Rustler was with him, and Winston was loaded for bear. What his plan was in tracking her mother and her would have been beyond Darby's comprehension.

As it was now, Edna stopped the tractor along a stretch of road where Darby spotted a patch of wildflowers growing. Darby wanted to pick flowers to take home to her family, and Auntie Edna could not refuse. Much to Edna's surprise was the discovery of pumpkins and pineapples growing nearby.

Edna twisted off a few pineapples and studied the wild pumpkins while Darby picked flowers. She decided to select one of the smaller pumpkins for Darby to bring home. It was small enough for Darby to hold in her lap while they finished the journey to Darby's house.

Edna listened to a shuffling noise in the roadside woods. Even though she did not see anything moving around in there, she yelled to Darby to get back on the tractor. Edna felt around her apron pockets instinctively relying on finding her Colt Pistol, but it wasn't there. She now remembered leaving it behind at the house. With no way to defend her and Darby, Edna dropped the pineapples and the pumpkin and scurried off to the tractor where Darby obediently waited.

"Sorry honey, but we have to go right away."

"But the pumpkin," Darby cried.

"Oh, there will be more of those old pumpkins in good time. I'll bring one when I come to visit, I promise."

Edna kept an eye on the forest as she started up the tractor and put it in gear. Soon they were safely away from the pineapple and pumpkin patch, and Edna eased back the throttle and went about a leisurely ride down the shoulder of the road. Dodging a few dead vehicles now and then, they sang songs and laughed at the dragonflies that darted back and forth between them. Sometimes a yellow butterfly would flutter by, and Darby would call out to the insect to land on her hand.

It could have been a sight for sore eyes, but the house Darby pointed to wasn't in the best of shape. In fact, Edna noticed that most of the south end of the house looked burnt, and though the house still firmly stood, it was in need of repair. Darby didn't seem to care or even notice. She was just glad to have come home. They rolled up to the porch, and Edna killed the engine on the tractor. "Marsha honey," Edna said with a tone of wariness in her voice. "Are you sure we're home?"

"Mommy must be out back hanging up clothes on the clothesline!"
Darby was off the tractor and running around the side of the house to the backyard area. There was an old Yugo automobile parked out back by the shed and barn, and Darby didn't seem surprised to see it, so Edna asked Darby who was home.

"Oh that's mommy's car," Darby said. "She must be in the kitchen."

They both entered the house through the back door that led into the kitchen, but no mommy. Darby broke away from Edna and ran into the living room, at which point Edna heard Darby shriek. Looking past the doorway, Edna saw a dark figure of a man sitting in a corner chair in the living room. Darby ran back and into Edna's arms. Being obvious this man was a stranger to Darby, she told her to go back to the tractor.

"I couldn't find the keys to the car," the stranger said. "But I'll take that tractor."

Edna glared at the stranger, "The tractor don't need no key. Take it and go."

The stranger bellowed forth an ensemble of laughter followed by a hoarse cough. He then informed Edna that wasn't going to happen, at least yet. "You see, I'm waiting for my kid to show up back here first and then we'll take your tractor and go." He then sighed, "The boy's been out running now for over a day, and I speck he'll be hungry when he gets back here. So I'd advise you get your ass in the kitchen and rustle us up something to eat."

When he got up and approached Edna, she noticed he had a gun in his hand. "So what's it going to be old woman?"

Edna turned and walked out the door and onto the porch.

"You step off that porch, and I'll put a bullet in you."

Edna didn't look back, but said, "I've got a picnic lunch on the tractor, and you're welcome to it."

As Edna strutted out to the tractor, she yelled for Darby to go back into the house. The stranger was watching Edna untie the picnic basket from the rear hitch of the tractor, but then looked back to Darby as she did what Auntie Edna told her.

The stranger mumbled something about eating the picnic lunch on the porch where they could see better in the daylight. However, when he turned a look back at Edna, he was faced with the maw of a white-hot blow torch just inches from his face.

"Is this enough light for you?"

The stranger threw his pistol over his shoulder as he instinctively tried to shield his face. Edna continued to hose him down with copious amounts of fire from head to toe. It didn't take long, perhaps less than five seconds or so. The stranger lit up like a tar-soaked telephone pole.

AFTERMATH

Darby started to run back, but Edna yelled to her to get back in the house and get a glass of water to help put the fire out. Darby did what she was told and returned as fast as she could with a cup of water.

The stranger pitched and rolled, screaming in pain. Edna dashed the cup of water out to help put out the fire but missed all three times. By now the man stopped crying and did more burning instead. Darby was wondering what happened to the stranger and Auntie Edna responded, "I was talking to him one moment, and then the next moment he just caught fire, honey!

I think we should better leave now. We'll send him some help if we run into anyone on the road."

"But Auntie Edna," Darby cried. "Can we come back?"

"Of course honey. Maybe tomorrow or the next day, we'll fix up a seat for Billy to ride in, okay?"

Darby squirmed in her seat, "I got a great idea, Auntie Edna. Let's take momma's car and that way Billy can ride in the back."

Edna thought about it a moment. She didn't foresee the need for the tractor in the next few days, and if there was space to put it in the barn ... "Well, I think that would be a splendid idea, Marsha. Do you know where the keys are?"

"Sure do. Momma keeps them hanging on a hook behind the bread box in the kitchen."

"Are you sure momma don't need the car for a day or two?"

Darby looked as if she was in deep thought for a moment. "I think momma and daddy went for a ride in the truck with Joseph."

"Oh, of course," Edna agreed.

The Yugo is a car built in the early eighties, were manufactured in Europe using the old technology of an electrical distributor, points and condenser. Having no electrical fuel injection, it had a carburetor instead and such needed no computer to run the engine.

Edna enjoyed the thought of being able to get home in less than half the time, and as they drove off, Darby begged to take Billy for a ride just as soon as they got back to Aunt Edna's house.

Edna smiled, "I am so looking forward to seeing Billy ride along with us too. We'll take him for a test ride just as soon as we get home."

Along the way, Darby was full of questions. "Why Auntie Edna, did that old man catch fire?"

Edna frowned and then cheerfully exclaimed that sometimes old men catch fire and that was the way things worked out. But then, she told Darby he'd be okay later on when the sun went down.

"Will my daddy catch fire when he gets old?"

"No, no honey. Only men who are strangers do that."

Darby smiled up to Edna, "Auntie Edna, you know everything!"
"Well I try honey, I sure try."
"I want to grow up and be just like you."
"Don't worry honey. One day you will be much smarter than your Auntie Edna."
"And Billy too?"
"Yes of course; and Billy too."

It wasn't that Edna ran out of nice things to say, it was just that some days the treachery of the way things are these days made traveling difficult. Up ahead a pair of roadside vagabonds was stepping out into the road, begging for them to stop or be run over. Edna figured that having a child in the car was tantamount to having to stop for whatever they had in mind. "Honey, I want you to brace your feet up against the glove box and push against it with your legs, okay?"

Edna knew the lap belt Darby wore was tight enough, but she didn't want to risk any injury nonetheless. "Honey we're going to play a game of 'Humpty Dumpty' who had a great fall ... "

Darby clapped her hands and doing what Auntie Edna told her to do she exclaimed, "I know that one ... Humpty Dumpty sat on a wall, Humpty Dumpty had a great – fall. All the ..."

Believing the car would stop was the biggest mistake this highwayman made as his lady friend watched him get smacked and then chucked over the roof of the Yugo. Amazingly, the car had only lost a headlight and fender in the challenge. Edna kept on driving while singing the Humpty Dumpty song with Darby.

Darby paused to ask, "What was that?" referring to the impact of the man being tossed over the car.

"Just another stranger," Auntie Edna said. Under her breath, she moaned, "They seem to be coming out of the woodwork lately."

Edna looked over to Darby and said, "How would you like to make a batch of cookies when we get home?"

Darby clenched her little hands together, "Oh Auntie Edna that would be so much fun!"

"And then tomorrow we'll drive back down to your house and see if your momma has come home."

They were entering the house, and Edna worried that she would forget where she put the car key when all at once she thought it would be a good idea to hide the keys behind the bread box just like Darby's mom did. "I'm so bad about misplacing keys," she told Darby, "so I'm putting them behind the bread box too. So if I forget where I put them, you can remind me okay?"

"Okay, Auntie Edna. Let's make some cookies!"

AFTERMATH

After a day like today, Edna was sure to get out her Colt Pistol or was it the Beretta, no matter. She had a choice of well over a dozen handguns, but she did like the weight and feel of the Beretta. The Ruger 9mm was a companion to the Beretta because they both used the same kind of bullets she knew. And after all, she had an ammo can left by her husband Sterling chock full of bullets for the two guns. She also had 7 other ammo cans but never bothered with them because they were just too heavy to tote around. 4 cases of slug fire shotgun shells and a mess of 5.56X45 NATO bullets for that wicked looking machine gun M400 Sig Sauer, her husband was proud of. He always insisted on having at least a dozen fully loaded clips in a canvas bag in the closet. Of course, he made sure she was familiar with the way it operated and how to pull the rifle apart for cleaning and so forth.

But Edna never felt she would need them, or have to rely on any firearm. But how things changed when it used to be hunting pigs and deer with Sterling, and now so much goes to waste. Edna nowadays felt it difficult to kill such a large animal for just her own needs and of course between her and Billy much went to waste in the garden. Sterling always planned on solar panels to help supply the house and freezers with the power they needed but fell on short notice when everything collapsed, and there was nothing left of money or resources. How nice that would have been she knew. However, Edna saw no sense on dwelling on things that could have been. So, in the end, it was the Beretta semi-auto pistol she tucked into her apron pocket. Making a mental note to herself was that since she was taking care of a child, it would be her responsibility to make sure she could keep Darby safe; and Billy too. She had plenty of other guns under her sofa, but she couldn't recall what kind they were. Maybe one day she would dig them out and take an inventory of them.

Pushing such thoughts aside, Edna checked the wood-fired oven to make sure the temperature was coming up evenly. Darby was still having fun kneading the cookie dough the way Edna had shown her when there was a knock at the door.

"Marsha, honey, there's a stranger at the door. I need you to go to your room and close the door."

Edna waited until she heard the bedroom door close before she went to the door.

Another knock.

"Speak up," Edna called out. "Who's there?"

After a long moment of silence and no reply from whoever was at the door, Edna said, "Go away. There's no way I'm opening this door, so go suck a lemon."

There was still no reply and just when Edna began to believe she had imagined the knock at the door, came another. "I said, who is it?"

Still no reply. Edna withdrew her Beretta and leveled it at the door in front of her. "If you don't speak up, I will have to look through the peephole in the door to see who's there."

A gruff voice finally answered back, "I don't see no fokin peephole!"

"Just a minute," Edna sang out, "I'll make one."

Edna shot a 9mm round through the door. She heard a grunt followed by a heavy thump of a body fall outside the door. She thought she heard someone scamper off the porch and run down the gravel driveway.

Edna pocketed her Beretta and walked over to the kitchen counter where she kept a drawer she fondly called her junk drawer. Seemed she never threw much away as inside the drawer was an assortment of wine corks. Taking out a paring knife she whittled down a wine cork small enough to fit the hole in the door. "Marsha, honey, you can come out now."

Darby tip-toed out of her bedroom, "Auntie Edna, what was that loud noise?"

Edna smiled warmly saying, "It was just a stranger at the door, and I had to shoo him away."

"But the loud noise."

"Oh yes. The stranger decided to shoot himself."

Darby's eyes widened, "With a gun?"

This was increasingly getting difficult for Edna. She wanted Darby to grow up in a world much like she did as a little girl her age. Violence didn't become her, and she tried to shield Darby from experiencing bad things. But the world was going through so much change that Edna feared those changes would continue and so she tried to make the best of it. Perhaps as Darby grew up, she would be able to cope with the horrors she'd experienced in a way that would temper her as a survivalist and not fall prey to the evil that continued to grow in the world today.

Edna was not naïve about what happened to Darby's family. She saw what happened to Darby's home and she struggled to put together an explanation in a way that the little girl could understand.

"Auntie Edna, why are you crying?"

"I always cry when I make cookies."

"I'm not crying, and I'm helping to make cookies."

Edna knelt down and gave Darby a big hug, "It's okay honey, and not everybody does."

Edna heard a sniff and pushed away gently, "Why are you crying?"

Darby's chin quivered. "I want to be like you."

AFTERMATH

Join me on Facebook: https://www.facebook.com/WriterTAWaters/

Sign up on my personal newsletter to better keep in touch for reports on new releases, book giveaways and other info: https://www.subscribepage.com/a2c1z2

Thanks for reading.

-T.A. Walters

Made in the USA
Lexington, KY
10 June 2019